WRITE, SHE SAID

Books by Jacqueline Gay Walley

'Venus As She Ages' Collection of Novels:
Strings Attached (Second Edition, Gay Walley)
To Any Lengths
Prison Sex
The Bed You Lie In
Write, She Said
Magnetism

Books by Gay Walley

Novels:
Strings Attached (First Edition)
The Erotic Fire of the Unattainable
Lost in Montreal
Duet

E-Books on Bookboon:
The Smart Guide to Business Writing
How to Write Your First Novel
Save Your One Person Business From Extinction

Amazon Chap-Books:
How to Be Beautiful
How to Keep Calm and Carry On Without Money

WRITE, SHE SAID

A NOVEL

Jacqueline Gay Walley

PUBLICATIONS

Book Five of the VENUS AS SHE AGES *Collection*

Many of these characters are based on real people, alive or dead. But this book is a work of fiction, because all the events and places got transmuted into a magical realism story that the real people would not the least identify with. In addition, just as many of the characters are fictitious, the events are fictitious, perhaps even my analyses in the books are fictitious.

Copyright © 2021 by Jacqueline Gay Walley
www.gaywalley.com

Published by IML Publications LLC
www.imlpublications.com

Distributed worldwide by Ingram Content Group
www.ingramcontent.com

Book cover design by Erin Rea
www.erinreadesign.com

Interior layout by Medlar Publishing Solutions Pvt Ltd, India
www.medlar.in

Cover Image: Alamy D884M3
Venus chastising Cupid
Contributor: Chronicle

ISBN: 978-1-955314-11-4

Library of Congress Control Number: 2021941312

IML Publications LLC
151 First Avenue
New York City, NY 10003

This book is dedicated to
Walter Staab for so kindly providing me with such
wonderful times in music, literature, and movies.
And helping me so much to live the life I am meant to.
There is no greater gift.

ONE

Oskar was making morning espressos for us by the window in his sleek machine that I have no idea how to use. The machine glimmers silver and seems to have as many stacks and towers as a power plant. The sun was weakly trying to come through his wall-to-wall penthouse windows. I was wearing the blue silk blouse and black skirt I wore the night before, since I would be leaving shortly to go to work, even if it is Sunday. He's a multi-millionaire and I am a pauper and that is how it is. I work all the time to stay broke.

"I read in the paper that writers are making less and less," he said, definitively.

Cheery news.

"It's over," he said. Oskar spends much time reading newspapers. *The Financial Times, Wall Street Journal, Investors Daily, New York Times, The Observer* all come to his door. I usually pick them up from his outside mat and place them on one of his antique chairs when I leave early in the morning. One day, he told me, "Put them on the table instead, not the chair." He is a particular man.

These directives of his don't seem to bother me. Maybe I enjoy being submissive for a few tender moments. Such a relief after all the aggression I am supposed to summon up to just get through a day in New York.

I looked at myself in his mirrored dining room, while he was busying himself with the coffee, and saw a woman who is not young. Very cheery news, indeed. I have been poor all my life but eked by. Now he's saying I may not even be able to do that. It's the day after my 59th birthday and I am already a little fragile. I used to be a vamp, a flirt, self-appointedly full of promise. Even I know I can't pull this off forever.

"Some people," I replied to his back, as I glared angrily at my betraying self in the mirror, "are making money through the internet. The Kindle. That type of thing."

"Yes and there are meteors out there, too," he called out over his espresso power stacks.

I watched him as he came toward me carrying his tiny ivory and gold cups. Here he is in an orange t-shirt, blue shorts, tall, slender, in perfect shape, "ripped" as he told the woman of the couple we had dinner with last night. Oskar works out 2 hours a day. Oskar, even though he is older than me, has no intention of getting old.

He is indeed "ripped," as he says, hence he has sexual power over me. I wonder if I were "ripped," if I would have sexual power over him. I am ripped, but not in the way he is. I am ripped inside.

He pulled out his blue exercise mat and began his 200 sit-ups while I sat down delicately and sipped my coffee. He said, "You would look better in that chair with the blue arm rests." I nodded, and continued sipping. I assumed he meant because of my blue blouse.

"I said," he repeated, "you would look better in that chair with the blue arm rests."

I moved to the blue chair. "This looks green to me," I said looking at the color.

"It's not. It's blue."

As I said, I don't bother getting upset with his strange obsessions and finickiness. "Don't play with your hair during dinner." "Don't kick your leg while talking." Why, my friends ask, do you put up with it? Why, my shrink says, do you respond only with confusion when something bothers you, not anger? I have no answer for this except maybe attention, any attention suffices for me. I am a motherless daughter. (I will save that story for another novel, one that I never want to write.) To continue. On why Oskar. Perhaps I want to engage with a man who forges some kind of power over me, rather than be with one whom I have power over. I have noticed that when I have a man jumping to my every move, I feel vaguely disgusted. (Doesn't he even have the intelligence of my mother to see I am not worth this kind of loving?) Or perhaps Oskar's behavior makes me feel awkward and vulnerable, takes me back to where all those feelings began and subconsciously I think I can begin again. I am new at love; I fool myself into thinking. My emotions are tentative, confused, larger than me. In other words, he makes me feel like a teenager.

And by rights, with his sexual proclivity of solely being taken with beauty, any kind of beauty—Iranian carpets, leather shoes, hatcheck girls of 17, young women with slender abdomens—Oskar should like that.

After the espresso part of our morning, he goes down to the exercise room on floor 3 of his high-rise building and I leave for my walk-up building in the East Village. He purses a cold kiss goodbye on my lips as he leaves the elevator, carrying a small DVD player so he can watch Juliette Binoche or Catherine Deneuve or Emmanuelle Béart or Marie-France Pisier while he treads.

I saunter by the doormen who, by now, know me. When they call up to him that I have arrived, they usually give me nicknames. That's because I used to make up silly names myself. I'd say, Tell him Second Avenue Mermaid is here, because Oskar calls me that. Or I'd use characters out of my own novels. Now the doormen themselves come up with boring names, like Snowflake, or Icicle (Nicicle would be better, Oskar says) and I let them come up with names because being a doorman must have more than its share of tedium.

As I walked out, I cursorily glance at one of the windows in Oskar's lobby that has sticking tape over it. Oskar told me the President of the Board of his building used a gun on the window to make a point to one of the doormen. Oskar says the Board President has "anger management issues," and then

Oskar laughs. At the condo board meetings, Oskar says the President puts his finger on each and every item on the agenda and says, "Let's move on."

I imagine Oskar's condo board as a present-day *Fawlty Towers*. It shows that the rich certainly have no warrant on sanity.

I grabbed a taxi in front of his building and, within minutes, I was at Second and Twelfth, where I get out and buy a coffee with milk, which I prefer, from the coffee shop next to my apartment and I climbed the stairs (that Oskar assiduously avoids) and I decide to open the letter from my agent about my new book, *Lost in Flatiron*.

The letter has been here since Saturday. Look, even I know, a letter is not a good thing. A good thing is a phone call saying, "I want you to fix the punctuation and some wrong names in places where you forgot to change the names that you changed 3 times."

Then I would ask, "Well do you like the book?"

The agent's response: "I love it."

That's a good thing.

I opened the letter. Dear Mira, Much as I wanted to love this etc., etc., etc.,

As Oskar stated, less and less.

I get that nervous feeling I get when I think I may not be able to take care of myself. You may be asking yourself, Well why doesn't she rely on her multi-millionaire boyfriend? This proves you have not had much to do with multi-millionaires. Let me tell you, it is the struggling people who stretch out a hand. They get it. Not all multi-millionaires are like him, I admit, in fact I have met some who do not defiantly align themselves with the 1%, who see money as a gift they have been given and one to continue giving. But Oskar is not one of them. It would be a fear of his to shield an aged dreamer. She should have thought of all this before, like everyone else does. Just look at what a mess the 99% get themselves into. How could they! Aesthetics! Ethereals! God! In fact, it is dawning on me that Oskar might not think about me much at all.

I put the agent's letter down, along with my hopes.

I was going to have to come up with something fast.

Amazingly, I did.

TWO

I was on 7th Street walking to Staples to return some printer cartridges, to get some kind of rebate that I never seem to remember to bring to the cashier when I do get them. It was cooling down now, November, and the street was dark. I looked in the window of a local bar to check out my lipstick color. This is a light color and I don't like light lipsticks but I keep trying to like them. In other words, I am trying to like my natural self. Of course, a dark window may not be the best gauge.

I looked in, expecting to see my familiar face, and instead saw a very old woman, perhaps 85, with soft grey hair, enormous intelligent eyes and a cupid mouth staring back at me. Her lipstick, may I add, was bright red, a decent color. She was wearing an ivory necklace, which for some reason tells me she is British. I suddenly realize she looks just like a woman I know. Exactly like her. Except the woman we are talking about is dead so how can that be? I have never personally met this woman whom I think she is, but I know her very well and I happen to love her.

I immediately dropped the cartridges in a nearby corner wastebasket so someone else could get the damn rebate and turned back toward the bar. I went in, and there sitting in a large velvet taupe chair is the exact replica of the writer, Jean Rhys. The opaque light of her martini is the only object transmitting brightness in this bar, although it's not brighter than the wit of her gaze.

In truth, she did not seem like a replica, she seemed like the real thing.

I had the temerity to sit down at her table, since I had all the confidence that I would be the only person around who would recognize her facsimile, the only person around who would think this was even possible. My sitting down at her table, I thought, would affirm her. I remembered my father, as he lay dying, saying to me that he could see spirits in the room. People kept appearing to him. Am I myself dying? I suddenly asked myself.

She smiled at me. "Well, I had to come," she said.

"Indeed you did," I answered, playing along. "You can't believe how hard it is to find a good book nowadays." I couldn't be dying; I had way too many unresolved problems for me to be dying. As if that makes any difference.

I motioned to the bartender that I would have what she is having.

She studied me with those translucent blue eyes that older Englishwomen seem to have, the kind of eyes where you can imagine where all those magical unicorn and fairy stories come from. She sipped her drink, her hand shaking. She put her drink down.

"You've got yourself in quite a mess, haven't you?" she said.

How the hell did she know? I nod, but not with shame, as I might with one of my well-heeled friends. No, I nod to this Jean Rhys or Jean Rhys look-alike, in conspiracy. The real Jean Rhys was a woman who specialized in making a mess of her life. I don't think there was ever a time when her life wasn't a complete disaster, financially, romantically, generally and specifically. A complete fuck up, as the Brits like to say, except for the sentences in the novels she wrote. They were never a mess. They were perfection. And, even better, unflinching.

"I have gone awry," I asserted, sipping my drink.

"I thought I'd help you," she said, rummaging in her bag for something. As if she'd been waiting for me. As if she is Jean Rhys.

Really? I thought. SHE, of all people, is going to help me? It seems she inflicted on herself all the same problems I do. Wrong men. Not enough money. How the hell would she help me?

I put my hand on her arm. "You can't smoke nowadays," I said. "Even I gave it up."

"It's interesting how the world consistently defaults to pettiness," she answered, putting her cigarette back in her purse. I could tell her she could smoke outside, but that did not accord in my mind. Jean Rhys hovering outside a bar door with a cigarette, as if she is an office worker—I could not see it.

"I don't really mind that it stopped me smoking," I said. "Anyway it ages you."

"You can see," she said, "how that might not bother me at this stage."

I smiled.

We sat in silence for a bit simply enjoying each other's company, she basking in my admiration for her, even if she was acting the part that she was alive again, and I sunning myself in this woman's audacity, whoever she is. The real Jean has been dead for about thirty years. Jean was a timid woman in life, hidden in drink and insecurities, but audacious in her writing. She took all that happened to her, all that could have broken her, and god knows a lot can break us, and she made art from it. My idea of a perfect woman.

And does she now have the audaciousness to come back to life?

"It goes without saying," I said, fishing in a way, "that I have read every one of your books, even *Tigers Are Better-Looking*, and, to me," I continued with a flourish, "they are incomparable. No one understood, like you did, how vulnerable a woman really feels."

She did something so unlike most writers today. So unlike our time of Lady Gaga and Beyonce's mother and god knows whom else. She ignored the compliment as if it was boring. Instead, she said, "Of course, what I did when I was broke and confused about life, was marry someone. I have never understood why you don't consider that."

I didn't answer because I didn't understand it either.

I ignored her and asked, "Do you remember that line in *Quartet?* '*She looked round her austere studio, and the Jewess' hunger for the softness and warmth of life was naked in her eyes.*'"

"Yes," she said. "You could never use the word Jewess like that nowadays." We both were quiet again for a bit while I tried to figure out what the hell was going on, and then she interrupted the silence with, "I wouldn't say that was particularly one of my better lines."

"Maybe not," I asserted, "but it spoke, it spoke to me."

"That must be because you must want some softness and warmth in your own life. I'm not saying I was any good at getting it myself. In fact usually not at all, I had married, as you know two men who went to prison and even the other one was a bit of a weakling. I mean we all are, aren't we, but we were sort of weaklings together in the same boat. In other words," and now she got a bit serious with me, "I let myself be had. This," she said, looking to her drink, "not withstanding."

She was reprimanding me for not being vulnerable enough. She meant I should learn to trust someone enough to give myself to them, to share my fate. Somehow she knew I have never been able to do that.

"Look," I said defensively, "I too have done my share of linking up with weak men, believe me, I just don't close any deals. I don't marry them."

"Because you don't want to be married."

"I do . . . and I don't."

"Well everybody," she said impatiently, "does and doesn't." I nodded.

Then I said, "Well, what was one of your favorite lines?"

"From that book?"

"If you can remember."

"Of course I can remember." Then she closed her eyes, and sat back and her skin was soft and so pale that it almost lit the dark and she recited, "*Still there were moments when she realized that her existence, though delightful, was haphazard. It lacked, as it were, solidity; it lacked the necessary fixed background.*"

"That's from *Quartet*, too," I said.

"I know," then she sipped her drink. "I don't know why I keep quoting from that particular book."

Well, she's so damn good at this that I think I'll just say she is Jean Rhys. Why the hell not? But even so, I didn't feel just now like talking about a "necessary fixed background." It was a topic I had managed to mismanage and I wasn't noticing any improvement in that area. "I think it's a bit late now for me to get married, anyway," I said, redirecting the subject.

"Well I don't think it's too late," she replied. "I was just about your age, one year younger I think, when I married my last husband. I outlived him but fortunately I was discovered in my late seventies, you know, for my books, so that kept me a bit busy . . ."

"I think you appealed to men more than I do."

"Nonsense. You turn them away all the time."

"So would you if you met the ones I meet."

She took another sip. "I wouldn't mind meeting them at all," she said.

And then she raised her delicate face, with her magnetic eyes upward and I followed them and there stood a handsome man. A bartender. Young, about 27, with dark hair falling over his forehead, a rakish way with his bar rag round his waist.

"You should be in an O'Neil play," she said sweetly to him, in her soft British accent.

"How do you know I wasn't?" he replied, smiling.

Jesus, nobody ever flirts with me like that.

He turned around to the bar and then back to us, with a drink for her. "I brought you a present," and she giggled and I swear she looked beautiful, eyes dancing, hair soft, a will of iron in the way she (or her character and who of us is not in some way some characters we've made up?) used what was damaged inside her, used it acutely. He saw it too.

"Lovely young man," she said as he returned to his post.

I nodded.

"So I think," she said definitively, "you should find someone and get married. You'll have other problems of course, but at least you'll have a friend and foe while going through it all. You know," she continued, "one gets interdependent as one gets older, and you, darling, are getting older."

I looked nervously around the almost empty room. Everyone around us was younger not only than her, but than me. I sipped my drink.

"So, I have come to help you," she said.

"Help me what?"

I studied her frail body, her old face, her gnarled hands with a very lovely sapphire and diamond ring. Who gave that to her, I wondered. My eyes then traveled to her old-fashioned beige shoes with heels, her beige stockings. I'll have to tell her the days of beige stockings are over.

"Change your luck, dear. I am going to teach you how to change your luck."

"Why not teach me how to write better?"

"I can't do everything. That you can do yourself by working at it. This, this you need more help with. You seem to be totally hopeless."

THREE

Oscar Wilde said that the only response to being poor is extravagance. I could not agree more. To live a life of abundance, no matter how your bank account disagrees with you, is to my mind like choosing to bob in the sun on the sea, rather than spend your time thinking about how easy it is to go under. Eventually we all do, so let's enjoy the sun while we can. So that's why I often take myself to the New York Philharmonic, or invite people out to lunch or dinner, buy myself flowers and CD compilations as I walk through Union Square. Why not enjoy the present with lots of presents? There are days that I tell myself to stop spending. Take the subway. Stop paying for people. But those are moments that disappear ephemerally, and I am back to my defiant behavior.

For this pleasure of profligate spending, I am constantly at my wheel teaching, writing silly articles, pretending I am interested in people's lopsided businesses, as I write about them.

So I was on my way in a taxi, rather than the subway, to the Philharmonic to hear Joshua Bell play a Sibelius violin concerto. I had invited a man whom I thought I might be interested in. Since Oskar keeps a distance from me, I often have my eye out for someone who will come in closer, and be foolish enough to marry me. But the man I took turned out to annoy me. Oskar, when he comes to hear music with me, usually has an avid eye, allows himself to enjoy the event one way or the other, even if he does fall asleep and ruin the whole thing for the people sitting next to him.

This tall thin man, the one I took instead, strode across the wide, lit up Lincoln Center plaza wearing a black suit and black shirt. Strike one. Did he really want to look like a vampire? He is a psychoanalyst so perhaps there is some connection. Then he insisted, as soon as we began walking together, on having a pre-concert coffee (Oskar, in a dashing suit, would have gravelly suggested a drink as if we were in a 40's movie). At this pre-concert coffee, sitting among countless old ladies munching on half a muffin, ladies who take their solace in music, as I already do and will be forced to continue to, my date wanted to talk about our relationship or lack of one.

"Why won't you tell me more about yourself? What you want . . ." he said. "Open up."

"What do you mean?"

"You don't tell me all your feelings."

"Really? You want to hear that?" I asked, nonplussed. In my mind, I hardly knew him. And why does he want to work on his off time?

My inner mechanisms immediately switched to those of a hunted animal's and I nervously began staring out the windows at the white Lincoln Center modern buildings that house centuries of exquisite music, ballet, opera. I looked at them frantically hoping they might provide me with an answer. Instead they made me think of their juxtaposition. Uninspiring exteriors housing incredible passion.

I turned to him, "Why don't we go sit down?"

Finally we seated ourselves in the grand and crowded concert hall. I read the program as I always do, to learn something rather than talk about something banal, and the psychoanalyst sat next to me looking around like a cormorant.

The conductor, once he raced onto center stage to great applause, stepped up onto his podium and then startled us by turning round to the audience and, rather than pay attention to the business of herding musicians, began to explain, as if we were at a graduate seminar, some of the upcoming modern music by a composer in residence.

"I don't like the conductor," the psychoanalyst whispered to me.

I nodded seemingly in agreement, while keeping my eyes coldly fixed on the stage. I didn't like this lecture much myself but refrained from mentioning it, because I believe in sometimes taking a rest from my critical nature. I save it up for the men I am with.

After the violin concerto was finished and Joshua Bell had taken his four encores, because let's face it, he does play exuberantly, the psychoanalyst in black said to me, "I thought the orchestra played too loudly."

I swayed my head from side to side, as if to say, Maybe. Actually, I thought the orchestra had played too slowly compared to Bell's violin dance but again I kept my mouth shut, to bask in the possible effect of taking in what was good. Most people aren't interested anyway in what you think; let's face it. They're interested in what they themselves have to say.

I also was angry at my date because he is quite attractive with thick grey hair that is as pretty as a woman's. I am mad at him for telling me all the vicissitudes of his current romantic life, which is another way of informing me I am not under consideration, even though I don't want to be under consideration. "I only see these people," he then burst out, "because I cannot wait for you forever." He knows I am faithful to Oskar. But if I am to leave Oskar, it will be for a man who insists on me, who will have no one else but me, who is overcome with passion. Not someone who is dating in self-defense. (Which was exactly what I was doing. But who wants to date oneself?)

So I left my music guest immediately after the concert let out, left him on the Lincoln Center piazza that was overflowing with music-lovers, left him standing by the gushing movie-set fountain. (What would Freud have to say about that?)

My parting remark to the psychoanalyst had been un-psychologically explicit, "I've gotta go." My last sight of him was he staring at me; stunned. I saw that inner child thinking, Why do they all run away? I felt a bit guilty but I precisely wanted to do that. Run away.

I settled into the back of the cab and began rationalizing. Doesn't he get it? I don't talk feelings, I write them. That is where they make themselves known, even to me. They're the plasticene I make something with on the page. In conversation, my feelings always feel a bit too plaintive, I told myself, too enormous in their longing. Who could possibly handle what I really feel? Maybe Jean Rhys could, but she herself put her feelings on the page. On the page, one can maybe refashion them.

I gave Oskar's address to the taxi driver.

The doormen called me up and Oskar had a fire waiting for us and he poured us both a scotch and he sat on a blue chaise longue in front of the fire, and I settled into my usual place of sitting on the hearth, my back to the fireplace.

"Mira," he said grinning, "where have you been? Give me details."

And I told him about the concert, leaving out the psychoanalyst part, and he nodded as he listened or pretended to listen, and then jumped up to play a new recording of a Mahler symphony since Oskar does like music, and calms himself with beauty. Then he returned to his blue chaise longue and we joked about people we knew, and he made a bit of fun of my poverty, which is his wont. "It would be good for us to go away, Mira," he said, "but the cost is astronomical in Italy right now. It's not like we're a two income couple, wouldn't you say?" It must make him feel powerful to point out my impecuniousness. But he does seem to keep me on my toes since I often forget about the need to be solvent and Oskar never does and so one of us has our eye on it.

Then we went to bed and took pleasure in just feeling each other's presence. I love the curly, strong hair on his slim chest and wide shoulders and how his body seems to be a perfect symmetrical fit for mine. It's true, he never kisses me and it took 3 years before he would put his arms around me but I have learned not to interpret this behavior as hostile. I interpret it as limited.

"What do you see in him?" friends ask. "He's so ungiving."

How can I explain that his selfishness and ineptness ensure me he is honest, at least about those parts of himself? That his quiet disdain, wit and unavailability are remarkably akin to the father who raised me. Where is the psychoanalyst when I need him?

That is the best I can give you. I am hoping against all hope that when I see Jean again, and I know I will because if she can show up magically once, it is a given that she will show up again (magic doesn't dally about with boorish concepts of aloofness or keeping a distance), I am hoping she will show me what the hell is going on.

WRITE, SHE SAID

In other words, I am clearly not making progress on the marriage front. She, on the other hand, met her first husband, Jean Lenglet, a convict-to-be, in a bar.

They were in England. Lenglet was handsome and attractive and most likely they met on stools that looked out at the bottles behind the counter. I could imagine the scene.

"You are so delicate," he would say, looking at her dancer's body. "Even your thoughts are," he flattered her. "You can't possibly be English."

"I'm from the Caribbean, from Domenica," she would answer, "That's why I drink this stuff, to keep warm. It's impossible in this country. Not only is there no sun here, there is no heating."

"Ah that's why you're so feminine," he mused in front of her. "You're like a girl."

She smiled, pleased. English women had been unkind to her from the day she arrived in England to go to boarding school. They thought her odd. She would like how he differentiated her from them. All artists like to be thought of as different. God knows why. Lenglet would appear to be listening to her with empathy, which was not what her British lovers did. Englishmen have a way of not paying attention to women, as if we aren't worth the trouble we bring. And the Englishman who had recently broken her heart was a stockbroker who probably had very little patience for the vulnerability of a woman who had no choice but to live in her feelings.

"And what do you do?" she'd asked Lenglet, this slight Belgian man who smiled cheerfully and generously. Who had already paid for her drinks and even suggested with flourish that they order dinner, a welcome surprise. He must be wealthy, she'd think. And he is not mean, like so many men.

"I'm in business," he'd say obliquely, since if one is going to eventually be intimate with crime, obliqueness is there from the beginning. It starts with an easy alliance with dishonesty.

"I thought you said you are a journalist," she would have said.

"I am that too." And he was, he wrote some articles well.

But whatever he told her, he probably obfuscated with great élan, which is something an artist cannot help but admire, for in some ways it is the work. But there is no question that she, who had an unerring ear for truth on the page, seemed to be most gullible in real life.

They fell in love till he left her stranded, broke. But he did love her. And she loved him. It was just he was as uncomprehending of how to manage in the world as she was.

She met her last husband at the funeral of a relative. He also was an about-to-be convict, an army man and solicitor, who was a cousin of her second husband. Another one who probably did not want to talk too much about his feelings. Perhaps poverty for both those men was too difficult to speak about or even feel, and so they took matters rather misguidedly into their hands. A shrink of course would say if they had spoken about their feelings, they would not have been led by their darker sides.

Her second husband was her literary agent. An unsuccessful one but devoted to her writing, and to her, because of it. They struggled, especially with her drinking and ensuing operatic dramas, but he did all he could for her, setting her up to write in Devon, allowing her to be devoted to it for all those years. Mostly she drank. Theirs apparently was a friendship love affair, not a lover love affair. Frankly, I myself can never abide a friendship love affair. I am a romantic, not yet so desperate, nor will I ever be, to want a man with whom I feign love. A friendship love affair, I am sure, is tinged with a seeping disappointment, and because of that, because of missing that rushing sea-swell of longing that a lover love affair has, a disappointment takes root that at times must feel violent. There are some who believe her neediness and selfishness killed that husband.

Should she be the one advising me on love?

I once heard a story of a woman who asked every man to marry her till she finally found someone who said yes. Of course, there was a time I could have got the sour psychoanalyst to marry me or at least I tell myself that. The psychoanalyst might have been loving if I had pretended I was and I might have arrived there in reality. That can happen too. You get used to trying to love someone so much that you think you do. But I have trouble being with someone. That is what Jean was saying. And she's right.

Just say yes, everyone keeps suggesting.

Alright. I'll try. I'll try and not fight closeness with every claw inside me. I'll try being the girl, and not being too intrepidly independent. I'll try going along. And if someone with a pure heart is fool enough to take me in, as Jean's husbands were with her, I will accept for a change.

Let's see, Jean, how that works out.

FOUR

The next day I read a friend's manuscript about a woman who joins a harem. It is true that women are in point of fact always joining harems. Past girlfriends, past wives, fantasized future girlfriends, mothers—they're all living vivaciously and clamoring in our lovers' minds. But somehow I wonder about her picking such a theme. Did the writer hope this theme would be possibly salacious enough to sell her work or does she wish she herself actually was in a harem and, like me, could give up the incessant daily decisions of real life that rarely live up to what one hopes? That said, I found the story dull since I find the difficulties of real life more than dramatic enough.

I was reading her manuscript in one of New York's old-tiled coffee shops with floor-to-ceiling glass windows where I intermittently looked up and saw hundreds of people rushing by, whenever I wanted to feel inconsequential. But the fact is I enjoy being by myself, on intimate terms with my warm coffee at a table with no one demanding conversation.

After that, I began to walk to meet a young writer friend; I mean very young, 13. He came loping toward me once I hit 23rd Street, his knapsack on his back. Already he is taller than me.

"Let's get some pizza at Eaterly," I said.

He nodded and we sauntered over to an entire building near Madison Square Park now dedicated to Italian food (Oskar buzzes in and out of there like it is his branch office. Oskar places much of his trust and interest in food). My young friend and I waited patiently for the pizza, hardly able to breathe as we were jostled this way and that by gibbering people pointing out this truffle and that cheese and that size radish.

Once we got what we went for, he and I left and grabbed one of the outdoor white iron tables and chairs that Bloomberg has put out now everywhere, the city slowly moving from its scrambling unceasing commercial focus to one of possibly being the kind of place that you can say, "Well we'll always have New York." It was warm for November so we spread ourselves out in the sun.

"I got a new video game," he said, while trying to balance his slice.

"Of course you did," I said, smiling.

I didn't tell him that I had noticed that his novel is now changing from its twelve-year-old focus on super power heroes to a thirteen-year-old focus on arighting vengeance. That tells me the narrative of his video games are changing, also.

"What's this one about?"

And he began telling me its plot, which sounded as complicated as *War and Peace*. He interrupted his recounting to add, "This is the second best pizza I ever had."

I laughed. At his age, he knows from whence he speaks.

I love this 13-year-old boy, with his handsome face and intelligent eyes, and his curiosity even about me, an adult, and his tremendous love of life which he betrays with the ultimate proof and manifestation of it: honesty. I wonder if he finds my admiration odd. Do his parents who allow me to help him with his opus (though they do pay me, but I buy him so many presents and outings and meals that this is hardly a pecuniary relationship) see me as a spinster with no children pathetically doting on their son or does he find some prurience in an older woman finding him delightful? I remind myself that I am his grandmother's age. And then that reminds me of all the men of 60 I know who feel perfectly acceptable flirting with girls 1/8 their age. Maybe I am more realistic about the outcome.

He took his bus back to the Bronx, after taking a brief spin, as he likes to do, in the corner comics store, and I walked in the unusual November sun and found a profusion of orange roses, and some French CDs and then plunked myself down in the sunlight to finish reading another friend's manuscript. Before I began, though, I decided to check my Blackberry. Oskar had emailed me to find out what we were doing tonight. We are going to the theatre with friends of mine whom he knows. And we are meeting for drinks at his Penthouse first. He never used to invite my friends over for drinks. Or do I only imagine this as increased intimacy? My trainer this morning tells me that I am wasting the last ten minutes of what's left of my looks on a man who does not want closeness.

Oskar has so endeared himself to everyone by being absolutely clear, as he would say, about the fact he is not in love with me. He will never marry me nor live with me, he says. I am of immense importance to him, he continues. Immense.

Everyone tells me our relationship is hopeless and some part of me knows it is true but what about the pleasure I take in his wit and handsomeness and masculinity? What about the freedom I have in his not adoring me? And who else has ever called me a Stradivarius in bed?

Give up, give up, that is all I ever hear from people.

But I also used to hear that about writing. And if I had given up, I would have had no life. No life at all. So using that syllogism, how can I give up Oskar, even if the returns are, as with writing, minute. Minute but a universe I am not unhappy in.

I was musing thusly when a woman asked me if she could sit down next to me on the bench where I was reading. I nodded and moved my flowers closer toward me to make room for her. Then I moved my coffee.

I continued reading, but studied her out of the corner of my eye. I could not believe this. There was no doubt. The stocky body. The dyed short brown hair. Another one with enormous eyes, although she was wearing glasses. Horn rimmed. A beige sweater set. A set jaw. Pugnacious. I bet even when she was young and pretty she was pugnacious. French women often are.

What the hell was going on in my life? Who would I see next? Socrates?

"Any good?" she asked nodding at my manuscript.

"Yes, the writer in the story has multiple personalities."

Marguerite Duras looked down at the pages. "What woman doesn't have multiple personalities?"

I laughed.

"Yes," she said. "You should add a few more to your own repertoire."

Maybe this was Revelations and rather than we people being called to heaven or whatever is supposed to happen, the dead are all returning and coming alive. I must read the Bible when I get home, I told myself. This was definitely Marguerite Duras, the dead French literary icon. Not even a facsimile.

I wished I had a cigarette (does just sitting next to someone French bring this out?) and then she pulled one from a silver case. She was holding onto a coffee, not a drink. She, unlike Jean, at least tried to give it up. Her liver. Although she was never able to stay sober.

Both my heroines who seem to have arrived on the scene were boozers. Jean wracked by booze, living in cold flats or broken down houses, with broken down men whom she tried to help prop her up, while she wrote. She drank for warmth.

Marguerite Duras, on the other hand, probably drank to cover what was hurt in her. Poverty in Vietnam, or Indochine, when she was there growing up with her proud destitute

French mother and her thieving brother. Marguerite, lonely with her intelligence, and burgeoning sexuality, alive sexuality, and nowhere to go with all this passion. It looked pretty doomed for her, and so soon drink came along to be her pal. She drank throughout the war, and later with lovers. It probably also dampened some of her ambition, not the ambition that all writers have, to get the work out, despite all, but the ambition to make a relationship work by dampening one's own needs. She had a long list of men and admirers, no question, but the trek, the trek was long. And the drink was constant.

"What kind of personality should I add to my repertoire?" I asked.

"A bold one, like your friend Oskar has."

"You need to be filthy rich to be that rude," I answered. Or have Asperger's.

"True. Why does he always mention other women to you?"

I had been wondering the same. "I know. This morning he brought up Baroness Veronique de Something, who is taking him to some black tie thing. Maybe to inspire me into jealousy or maybe he's just honest about what he does . . ."

"I wouldn't worry too much. Other women will want him to connect," she said, "which will terrify him. He doesn't want to feel." So she knows. How is it that she knows? I was amazed at how quickly I was taking to the supernatural. I always thought it odd that people liked movies about what was clearly unbelievable. And now here I am accepting the impossible as if it is a Fresh Direct delivery. As they say, we are a species who adapt. Except to the problems between our genders.

"I don't know," I replied. "I think he is changing. Slowly."

"Maybe," she said, smoking, looking at the people passing by. Boys with knapsacks. Women pushing baby carriages. "You should meet a man who is in love with you. He clearly isn't. Or can't be."

"Yes," I sighed. "I know."

"Hard at your age, I admit it. It got enormously difficult for me as I got older. I never met anyone and I was famous. *The Lover* put me on the map."

"I know. That book was marvelous."

She cocked her head at me. "It's everyone's favorite. Why? Was it yours? It's not mine . . ."

"The simplicity," I said. "You wrote a whole family construct, a whole colonial construct, a whole desperate love construct, an artist as a young woman in construct, in what 100 pages . . .? The economy of the sensuality in the writing made it devastating . . ."

"I suppose," she said, sadly.

"Well I am not giving you bad news," I said, smiling. "It was irrevocable."

"Yes. Funny how it took me till almost 60 to write it."

"It takes almost that long to do anything. I don't know why . . . Maybe if one is a woman who feels so much," I said, "one is blinded a bit. So much to take in. It's overcoming and confusing to sort out. It takes years to have any idea of what actually happened to you. Why one does what one does. What one should do next . . .?"

"Some never do figure it out," she answered. "But I think you can. I even think you can meet someone who will make you happy. With my help."

That again. These women are insistent. And why are they helping me, I wondered. Was a returning Dickens arriving right now in Los Angeles to help Robert Ludlum? He didn't seem to need much help. Tolstoy must have come and gone in helping David Grossman, his last novel had the Russian genius' imprimatur. Who is Virginia Woolf with right now? Anyway that these two writers chose me is a wonderful compliment. I mean they both were difficult women who were impossible in their love lives (although at least they had them, but I have had them too, lots of them, it's just now I have got myself in a mess, and it's not really a mess, I just happen to be fixated on a man who does not seem gaga over me) and these women were hurt, hurt, hurt, and that was much of what they wrote about, like me, so I guess that is why these two have picked me, I told myself.

I then turned to Marguerite. "Which book was your favorite?" I asked.

"I don't remember," she said impatiently.

"*Emily L.* was my favorite. The woman poet, whose Captain husband co-opts her for himself. She doesn't know her work has become well known. He's got her lost in drink and at sea literally." I suddenly wondered if I wanted someone to co-opt me. I was speaking so longingly. Then I began to quote the book to Marguerite: "*'You don't move at first, then from where I'm sitting I can see a smile in your eyes. You say, 'You like this place. One day it'll all be in a book—the square, the heat, the river.' I don't answer. I don't know. I tell you I don't know in advance, or only very rarely.'*"

Marguerite was not impressed with my recitation. She was looking away.

I looked away too and reflected on why I liked *Emily L.*, of her books, the best. In truth, I had been co-opted by a Captain, also. My father, the Colonel. He had been so possessive of me as a child (perhaps that is why I interpret love that way and Oskar comes up wanting) that my mother, when she wanted to leave, just thought it a given that I would go with him (or more likely she didn't want her children, I don't know). He took me out of schools, away from friends, so I would be completely devoted to him and his drinking in seaside towns.

Once I said to him, "Well you just want me to be in bars sitting next to you all my life. That is what you want for me."

He turned to me and said, "What's wrong with that?"

He, like *Emily L.'s* husband, was not interested in what poems lay inside me. Perhaps my father was interested in poems that lay crumpled and strewn all over the beach or the bar, illegible from the elements and neglect. Perhaps he saw those. But I doubt it.

Then I began thinking I should mention to Duras, as she sat beside me, how Jean Rhys also wants to help me now. Maybe they had known each other. They had both lived in Paris but Jean was older and in a different crowd than Marguerite. Jean kept to herself. Her husband had been in the jail, La Santé for illegal currency trading, when Jean was living in Paris. She was waiting for him to get out. Broke. And of course having an affair with the man who had taken her in. But writing. Writing. And then ended up back in England.

I was born in England of a drunk father, a colonel in the British army. Or so he said. Being born to a drunk father eventually, by necessity, turns into a kind of war.

Marguerite was busy in the war, in the resistance seducing Germans as a decoy, and afterwards, writing novels, films, articles, a bit of a star.

During the war, Jean's first husband was in a concentration camp for his activities in the Dutch resistance. He survived. Marguerite's husband was in a concentration camp for his activities in the French resistance. He survived, just.

I was raised in Montreal on French writing, and its resistance to the bourgeoisie, its resistance to the American insistence of sameness in love, and this is how I kept myself, when young, from breaking down.

The two women will have to get along with each other if they are planning on living with me, as they seem to both be doing, now that they are back from the dead.

I turned to Marguerite and said, "I am surprised you want me to meet a man. I would have thought you would have wanted me to focus on my career."

She turned to me and said, "I AM French, darling."

FIVE

Oskar's world is very small. All his energy is made up of attending to himself, although I am not sure that those words could not be said about most of us. He has an enormous portrait of himself with his dog (who has since died) sitting over his fireplace. He refers to himself in the third person sometimes and has told me many times what a creative genius he is. He is much younger looking than his 65 years and he does indeed have a perfect physique. That is not what draws me, as pleasant as it is.

What I like is that he has had to work harder than other people to understand the world since his precise and detailed mind craves order, and this has given him a curious attentiveness, a selectivity of what is good in life which has been thought out and hence not unintelligent. But what I really like is that he is often surprising. However, he is not as intelligent as he thinks he is, hence when I brought Jean over, he did not know that she has come back from the dead.

He has not read her books, which is astonishing to me since he is quite literary.

"Why that should astonish you I don't know," she said to me, as he handed her a scotch in a crystal glass. "Plenty of people have not read my books. Only literary people read my books."

Oskar bristled a little since he thinks of himself as literary. He does not know what he does not know, so he thinks he knows much more than he does. If you can think of a compliment, he would apply it to himself, child-like, without any conflict.

We three sat outside on his wrap around terrace and Jean took in the city of New York, which glowed, orange in the evening sun. He pointed out planes landing at Newark, the Flatiron building, and the usual sights that people not from New York are struck by. She did not comment. Most people ooh and aah over his terrace but then she has already died and gone to heaven and come back so what is a damn view to her?

I sat on his blue cushions looking out over the city and as the sun began dying, a sliver moon, as if we were in a fairy tale, rose in the sky and began to shine. For some reason one of Jean's lines in *Wide Sargasso Sea* came to me. Perhaps it was the night sky looking like a sea, and my emotions, as I sat on the terrace, feeling like waves. Jean had written, *"'Do you think that too,' she said, 'that I have slept too long in the moonlight?'"*

I turned my eyes back to Jean, pretty, in pearls, wearing a French gardenia perfume that smelled as if we had walked into a magical garden and as I noticed it, Oskar began coughing.

"What's wrong?" I asked. He had already refilled her scotch on the rocks.

She was looking rather pleased. "Is it the perfume?"

"No," he said, "something caught in my throat."

Jean turned her gaze to him.

"You're very attractive, aren't you?" she said to him.

"I take that as a compliment," he said, puffing up as usual.

"What are your feelings about Mira?"

"I think Mira is very valuable property," he replied, smiling at me.

"What on earth does that mean?" she asked.

I was wondering the same.

Jean was thinking. "She is an artist, and they can do some interesting things as you know. Have you ever thought of investing in the arts?"

At this point I wanted to jump off the balcony.

"I am continually," he said, "giving her ideas to make money. I want her to make money."

"What kind of ideas?" she asked.

"Commercial book ideas."

"God how ridiculous," she said. "No one, not even the publishers, can ever figure that out."

"Well I can," he said, smiling provocatively at her.

"How fortunate to be so prescient," she said, sarcastically.

"Yes," he replied, a bit confused. His swaggering wasn't working on her.

"Why is it important to you that she makes money?" she asked.

"So I won't feel as guilty."

Jean took another sip.

"And," he said, "she will be happier."

"I don't think you love her," Jean said.

"What is love?" he asked.

"I am sure you can recall," she said.

"I can. And it got me nowhere. You don't see me with any of my so-called passionate loves. I prefer now a sane relationship because I suspect it will last longer."

"There is no such thing as a sane relationship and anyway who would want one? People want intimacy with all the inherent pleasures and, of course, difficulties of that."

Very good, Jean, I thought.

"I am trying to avoid difficulties," he answered.

"You mean," she said, "you are trying to control difficulties."

He said nothing.

"Believe me," she said, "you won't. They are uncontrollable and you will only render resentment with your control."

"This is a strange turn of conversation," I said.

Oskar looked from her to me and back to her and then made a face as if to say, Is she crazy? It took me years to know that people who do that are the ones who might be crazy.

She, on the other hand, gazed at him with her blue eyes that really had more color than the entire New York skyline.

It all made me think of what William Trevor had written about her: "*Jean Rhys, who never put a foot wrong in her writing, rarely put one right in her life. She was probably not more disaster prone than most people, but she did not dissemble and although she hated ridicule and spitefulness she exposed herself to both: she lived as she wrote: honestly."*

Oskar really didn't have a chance with her lack of dissembling because, of necessity, dissembling was his game. They nullified each other out.

And then I looked at her again and I thought here is where an artist is someone so voluble, so spot on, because this is when she chose, once again, to say nothing.

But she did say, "Perhaps you are not over your last girlfriend."

"Perhaps I'm not."

I like that he is honest, even if it is bad news for me.

We chatted about banalities from thereon in, or rather, he did and I thought she was just trying to show me how impossible the situation is. I thought she was pondering what we should do. Look for someone else or come up with a strategy for him.

"You should go somewhere with Mira," she said. "Do something romantic."

"The dollar is weak," he said.

"I wouldn't say it's the dollar," she answered, sipping her drink.

Suddenly she stood up, in her beige silk dress. "Pass me my canes," she said, to me.

I got up and fetched them from where they were waiting sentry-like at the door. I handed them over to her and she said, "I'm going to the theatre, so we must go," pointing at me with one of her sticks.

Oskar never minds being left alone. Anyway he isn't left alone. He has a young French girl, who is his chef, living with him. They both spend their time reflecting on the perfection of their bodies and their clever ways of attaining and maintaining such epidural invincibility. Like teenagers.

In the elevator going down, Jean said, "I don't know if you would like being with him if you spent more time with him. He knows that and that's why he keeps a distance. Yours is not," she added, "a relationship built on the sympathique."

"Well we get on."

"Yes but not that well. I don't see union. You don't talk together. Does he know anything about what you write? Does he care?"

Now I was silent.

"No union at all," she added.

As we left the elevator, she said, "I don't know if he's worth it, even if he is inordinately rich. You don't have forever you know."

It was odd my having linked up with an impaired man. Not that odd, really. I had been involved with many other emotionally impaired men who all seemed to get better once they were with another woman. I had taken to these men when they were sort of jigsaw problems to me in their feelings and expressions. I became fascinated with the lexicon of their jumbled, wounded emotions. I would decode them endlessly, encouraging their impossibilities, fooling myself, and them, that all their idiosyncrasies were individuality. In other words, I spent time "in the head," which, according to Winnicott or the *Drama of the Gifted Child* woman, is where the unloved child soothes him or herself. It is not safe to feel, it is better to think.

It was always another woman who straightened my lovers out, once the other woman got her hands on them. In other words, they were artistic problems to me that I wanted to solve. Other women turned them into men and enjoyed the benefits of that. Probably by loving them with feelings, not treating them as diagrammatic puzzles. So all I ever got, which was I guess what I got as a child, was the continual touching of the aching missing tooth, not love.

Jean Rhys and I were still walking through the lobby as this went through my mind.

"But you know," I said to her, "he can't be that impaired since he has made a success of his life. He may not be emotional or loving but he's not a total loser. Maybe his concreteness appeals to me since I am too much in the clouds."

She said nothing. I remained silent too because I found myself thinking, And here I am running into women who are allegedly permanent residents in the clouds.

"Darling," she said, "you can have more than that."

"I hope you're right," I said.

"I am. Just want it. Desire it. That's the first step. Then somehow," she stopped for a bit, "it usually presents itself."

Is that true? I wondered.

As we made our way through Oskar's lobby, she began studying the doorman, Gino, whom I do have to admit is quite attractive. Tall, Italian, with a sense of humour.

"Isn't he lovely?" She said, as we walked by slowly. She gave him a megawatt smile and he returned it and she said to me, "That is how it is done."

"What?"

"You initiate. You respond. You invent. You participate."

Gino at this point had raced to open the already open door for her. He stood there gallantly, she looking up at him with all the sweetness of a 16-year-old girl.

"Will you be returning soon?" he asked her.

"Well, I wasn't planning on it," she said, "but now I will reconsider."

"That is wonderful," he replied and she giggled.

When we finally reached the outdoors, as if she was exhausted, she said, "Let's sit down."

There are stone seating areas that border the red impatiens plantings outside Oskar's building. "I do wish I could meet someone now," she said. "Love is such a wonderful way to spend one's time . . . I do wish it."

I looked at her in her 80s and was confused as to what to reply.

"Well," I said, "judging by the way you attract people, I think it's inevitable."

"Yes," she said, standing up. "Same goes for you," she added. "I'm going off. Get me a taxi."

She took quite a bit of time getting into the cab, but get in she did and, out of respect, I did not ask where she was going. But I knew she would return to me. More surely than I knew Oskar ever would.

SIX

I walked in to my apartment and there lying on my PC was a ticket to Vienna and Prague leaving two days from now. And a note: "We're going with you. You really should see these cities. We've made all the arrangements. You need to open your mind to new adventures."

I didn't need to be told who the "we" were who had left the tickets. It was curious that these two had come back to life at the same time. I mean if anything is possible, as Oskar likes to say, and here this is being evidenced, why did Jean and Marguerite come as a matched set? Maybe they themselves didn't want to be aliens, as Oskar calls himself, alone in this world that they would now be unfamiliar with. Maybe they knew they were writers of the heart and how the heart breaks and it would be too much brokenness for them to come and be reminded of all that by themselves. Maybe now they knew enough not to be that unkind to themselves anymore.

I held the air vouchers in my hand and ran my fingers along the edges. There was no doubt about it; the tickets were real. How remarkable. But why me? There was of course the insistent fear behind everything that I myself am dying and they are here to act as Charon on the River Styx. And if that is not the immediate case, then why have they chosen me out of all the writers, so many of us now, clicking away at laptops, even phones? I decided, and perhaps this speaks more of my personality than truth, that they chose me because I was a particular brand of nomad, like them. I was not an intellectual in the Upper West Side academic sense. I had always been on the margins, hurt, a stranger in a strange land, like they (émigrés), rejected by parents, longing, longing for love, and this, this had been our material. Also their careers were saved at the last minute, and so perhaps they chose me for that hopeful ending. Who knows, as King David said? But I looked down at the tickets and thought where else should I be except with my two heroines on a journey?

Two of Marguerite's lines in *Emily L.* . . . suddenly floated before me: "*I looked at them. And said, 'Loving as a form of despair.' You smiled, and I smiled back. 'Running away from everywhere like criminals.'*"

But Jean, Marguerite and I were not criminals. But we were indeed running away from a crime. The crime of having chosen to not be loved in a sustaining way. The crime of all three of us not being related enough to reality. Or only being related on the page. Maybe if we were alone together, in a new place, we would come alive in new ways. That must have been their thinking.

Jean called me and said, "What does Oskar think of our going?"

"He thinks it's old fashioned. Three women off alone like this." Actually what he really said is that I am insane. If he knew these women were dead, I think he would have come with the little white wagon with those doctors to get me.

"Isn't all this your imagination?" he asked.

"Isn't everything?" I answered. "It's my imagination that makes the movie house across the street more vibrant a building to me than the apartment building next to it. It is my imagination that dons everyone walking by with different textures than how others perceive them. It is my imagination that misreads most of my relationships and misreads my own strengths and weaknesses."

"He's just jealous he does not have close relationships," Jean said to me on the phone.

It didn't ring right to me. He has some close relationships, his son, his chef, his ex. The bevy of women he is seducing at the tennis club.

"He told me," I said, "that he is going to be seeing some other Baroness while I am away."

"What an idiot he is," she said. "It's sickening."

I knew it was true but I wanted to protect him. "I think he said it as a child does. I will go play with that person now. I don't think it meant much."

Nothing from her.

"I don't really mind," I added.

"Don't be ridiculous," she said and hung up.

SEVEN

"How are we going to pay for this?" I asked, as the concierge, the bellman, the waiters rapidly began treating us as royalty. Marguerite had booked us into a 5-star hotel in Prague, the Aria.

"At this point in my death I am not going to worry about money. God will provide."

I smiled at her. Did she mean literally?

Jean was checking out the bar.

We each were put in different rooms that had musical names. Jean was in "Verdi." Marguerite in "Showtunes" (ridiculous since she is hardly Oklahoman, this stolid woman who had the moral consciousness to write *Hiroshima, Mon Amour*) and I in "Hard Bebop" (not as ridiculous, I do like jazz). We were jet lagged and had a breakfast, then a lunch, then a short walk to the Frank Gehry building with its tin colors and top hat of a circular globe and cold windows and strange swerving front. It sits over the river, ultra modern, a contortion next to the elegance of the Prague Renaissance, Gothic, and every other type of gorgeous building. Everywhere we looked we saw granite and soapstone sculptures, windows, stone, stone, stone. Trees, roses, red leaves. Gardens.

"What are you thinking about?" Jean asked me as she hobbled by the Brno River, over the grey of the water and under the grey of the sky.

I looked at her and said; "I am finally understanding why you two brought me with you."

"Which you think is what?" Marguerite asked impatiently. She tended toward impatience, a sign of many geniuses. She was walking brusquely, in flat brown shoes, a pencil skirt and sweater. Her hair was blowing but since it was short, it moved just a little. Her glasses reminded me of the windows in these exquisite stone buildings in that they seemed to hide political strengths, sufferings and centuries of artistic beauty.

"Havelock Ellis put it best," I answered. "He said, '*Finally, it may be observed that the atmosphere into which genius leads us, and indeed all art, is the atmosphere of the world of dreams.*'"

"What are you trying to say?" Jean laughed.

"That you want me to let go. You want me to let imagination win. Even in my own life."

"Exactly," Jean said. "Imagination and beauty. If you have an image, then it really is sending you a message, an image to go for. Go toward it and stay with it. It will lead you to the right place."

They suddenly seemed to be peering about as if they were ship captains.

"What are you doing?" I asked.

"We're looking for men," Marguerite laughed. "We miss them."

"I know," Jean said. "We should have a love affair before . . ."

I nodded agreement, god knows, we all should have a love affair or two before . . . and I too began scanning but my eyes only saw the cathedrals on the hills and the little bridges and I felt I was in a Grimm's fairy tale, not a dating landscape. After all, I was surrounded by fairy godmothers.

Marguerite was uncharacteristically smiling.

"Does she see something?" I asked Jean. "Marguerite looks so happy."

"No." And then Jean whispered, "She liked when you referred to her as a genius. In the Havelock Ellis quote. She always liked that."

We came back to the hotel because it was starting to rain and we went to our rooms to rest and then met for dinner. But beforehand we were to light Shabbos candles together since it was Friday night. Marguerite had brought them in her bag. In fact, she always had crackers, chocolate, medicines, endless surprises inside that brocade sack she carried with her everywhere. But the reason for the Shabbos candles was that since she has died, she has converted to Judaism, which is not surprising since when she was alive, she wailed and screamed in horror at the Holocaust. After all, her own husband, Robert Antelme, was imprisoned as a political prisoner, starved and tortured, with the Jews, and she went to all those train stations after the war, looking for him, not wanting to give up. And she saw what she saw. After that, the Jews, to her, were indeed the chosen race. They had meaning.

She waited and waited and finally someone mentioned that they had seen Marguerite's husband, a man whom everyone admired for his conscience. He was alive, they told her.

When he was in the camp, they told her, he had consistently discussed philosophy and ideas, she was told, to help others. Marguerite could not believe they had finally found him. She was so happy. She dispatched his friends to go get him, once they located where Antelme was, and drive him back to Paris. But Marguerite, they said, be prepared.

When she finally saw her husband, she ran to her bathroom and hid. Doctors told her he would die. She however kept searching for a doctor who would not agree, and eventually found one. He was Indian and knew how to treat starvation. He slowly brought Robert back to life.

It took weeks before her husband could hold his head up to be fed. He drank liquids under that Indian doctor's care. Meanwhile, she was hearing everything that happened from friends, from those who also went to wait at train stations, she was untiring in what she insisted on knowing.

She was deeply in love with her husband's best friend and it was he and she who lay him down on the couch and nursed her husband back to health. Who was sleeping with whom was of no interest to anyone at that point.

Her last books were about the irrevocableness of that pain, her stories about Jewish orphaned children, there was no turning away in her mind from what happened.

"While we're here," Marguerite said, "I want to go to the Jewish quarter."

Jean rolled her eyes. "The Jews," she said, "always the Jews."

"Precisely," Marguerite said. "But I have my reasons."

That was when this French woman, probably Catholic when she was alive, pulled out 3 Shabbos candles for us, and we each lit a match and lit a candle before dinner. Jean said she didn't know what the hell was going on. I smiled to myself at how the British often don't want to know what is going on in other cultures.

Marguerite said the prayers in Hebrew and then added, "This is amazing we are together." At which, we each one almost started to cry. This impossible meeting, this dream, as Havelock Ellis would say, was extraordinary, Shabbos candles or not.

"It is wonderful," Jean agreed, "to be alive and with each other like this, isn't it. After all, life can be lonely."

I wanted to say, Death must be too, evidently.

I nodded. I felt like crying it seems for all the same reasons that they did. Meaning we were all rather struck at the absolute shock of this being here now in this gorgeous city, in this gorgeous hotel, each feeling close to the other. As if we were bonded on a ship going somewhere we did not know but we were committed to each other on the journey.

After we had finished the Shabbos prayers, we went to the Blue Duckling down the street for dinner. Had scotch, wine and vodkas, delicious duck (the Eastern European countries know how to cook meat) and just ambled in our conversation. Nothing serious in our dialogue just the warmth of being three people who wanted to live well, enjoyably and love. Such generosity.

But I saw what was really going on. In being treated well, and loved, I was being changed.

I saw how Jean put her hand so warmly on Marguerite's arm when I asked about Paris.

"I was never able to sell my writing there," Jean said.

Marguerite said, "Well, I had problems with Gallimard."

Jean said, "I wish I had had problems with Gallimard. Ford Madox Ford was the only one who could get my books published in England."

"Well you're both published everywhere now," I said.

"Are you?" Jean asked me.

"Just two books in the States," I answered. "Have you read them?"

"We're like young people nowadays," Jean said. "We don't read."

Marguerite said, "She's joking. We've read them."

Jean said, "Of course we have. Why do you think we're here? I liked the first one where the girl is so lost and fights back."

Marguerite said, "I like the second one better. More adult. The second one is colder, more about longing for love."

"Is that why you chose to be with me?"

And I have to say what happened is that they did not answer and began mentioning some man in Paris, whom they both knew, and that led to another man and soon they were mocking these people, but more for humor's sake than anything, more to just have fun, and I saw that that connection is all to live for and I saw that nobody wants to be marginalized, not even after death, and I saw that giving, that aristocracy of the soul, begins a healing. I saw that beauty and friendship and caring are everything, as well as being alone, which Oskar loves, and I do too, and so do these women, but I saw that I had made a commitment to them. And they to me. So what if they are dead or temporarily alive, as they seem to be, as I am for that matter? We had made a commitment to be together on this trip.

"Tomorrow," Marguerite said, "you will see why your mother left you."

"For people like us," Jean said, "there is always something more to rewrite."

EIGHT

It is a funny thing to go sightseeing with two fiction writers, never mind two deceased fiction writers, but either way.

Anyway, there we three were at the Prague Castle and we didn't pay much attention to this architecture being Baroque and that wing being Gothic and this building a perfect rendition of Romanesque. We didn't pay much attention to the formal dinner sets of dishes or the Czech glass of the former Prague monarchy, Charles the Second, who seems to have been quite benign creating a university and gardens open to the public and the like.

We noted the greyness of the day and each of us had an umbrella and were abnormally concerned about being warm. Jean's umbrella was unusual and could double as a seat when she wanted to rest.

Marguerite said, "We have a lot to see today. It will make you understand," she said, "where your instability started."

I wasn't enchanted with this description of myself but who am I to argue? And anyway I already knew why I was skittish. It was not going to be any revelation.

"Look at this," Jean said when we were standing next to where the Prague crown jewels were locked up in a vault with 7 locks, using 7 different keys, each one being in the hands of 7 different dignitaries in the Prague government.

The guide explained it to us. Once a year in Prague, the dignitaries put the crown jewels on display for the public. We were looking at the replicas of the jewels but one could still see these were serious stones, outdoing anything Elizabeth Taylor got her hands on. At least to my inexperienced eye they seemed to be. My two women friends didn't seem particularly savvy about jewels either, more the type to receive odds and end pieces of jewelry from lovers whose finances were at odds and ends, too. But we all three got inspired about what could happen if someone wanted those jewels.

Just the number seven was a trigger to our imaginations. The word "locks" and "keys" were sort of launching pads too.

"Perhaps because we're women," Jean said. Marguerite laughed.

"Do you really miss sex so much?" I asked Marguerite.

"Of course. Why wouldn't I? There is no greater happiness than sleeping next to a man you love. Touching him. Kissing his skin. No greater sense of wholeness."

"Maybe you two will meet someone you can love on this trip," I replied. If their being alive was possible, so could that possibility be. However, I wondered which was least likely—resurrection from death or meeting a man when you're over 60.

"What happened to the jewels when the Nazis were in power?" Jean asked our Czech guide, Marta.

Immediately Marta got excited, taking a few steps out ahead of us and shouting in her husky voice. "The top Nazi official, Heidrich, situated himself at the Prague Castle, like all the governors and Presidents do . . . Of course he wanted the jewels for Germany."

"Did he get access to the 7 keys?" Jean asked. As she stood there, her frail body seemed to be quivering with energy.

Our blonde guide, Marta, was emphatic. "Of course he felt the Germans would win the war and so he was sure the

Germans would get the Prague jewels, eventually. He did keep on with the ritual of displaying the Prague jewels annually to the citizens, to show he was not being unkind to the Czech peoples. But of course the Nazis were after the jewels; they were after everything. It was a mania with them, land, countries, money, power . . ."

Jean and Marguerite nodded their heads, and then, eyes gleaming, looked at each other and then me.

All of us felt the ignition.

"This would make a marvelous story, let's face it," I said, "the story of how the Prague officials deceive the Nazis so they can't ever get them, even if the Reich won."

"Yes there was another story," Marguerite said, standing sturdy and sure in her pale raincoat that she had buttoned up to the top in that officious manner of hers, "about the Polish gold which was run out of Poland on a train, by students, a madcap story. The gold made it to Switzerland."

"They're almost as bad as the Nazis with keeping things," I said.

Marguerite said to me, "They are not as bad as the Nazis were. No one was."

I tightened my cheeks, chastised. Alright, that was a stupid statement on my part. But she too is forgetting that she is notorious for possibly having had a relationship of some sort with a Nazi. Of course, it was to get information, as part of her Resistance activities, but Mitterrand, all of them knew, she was getting some frisson out of the endless lunches, dinners, meetings with her Nazi, who was taken with her. Few women don't like being taken with.

I did not feel judgmental about her flirting with a Nazi since I had in my life been attracted to a sadist once or twice myself. You can't corral sexual attraction. And in the end she set him up to be killed. I was never that intelligent in my own relationships. It was I who got wounded.

As we continued walking, our Czech guide revealed that when the Russians had been there, she had been a dissident. She told us how she and her dissident friends could only live outside Communism by waiting every Thursday to buy contraband Western books translated into Czech—and that was their window into freedom.

"You know," I said, "who these women are?" I pointed to Jean and Marguerite.

And it was so exciting, once I made the introductions. Marta knew Marguerite Duras' work, *The War* and *The Lover*. She did not know Jean's which made me sad. Jean was a writer's writer, I was finding out. Not everyone knew her. And it was really unfair since she was as good as Marguerite any day. My heart began to break, because in truth I considered myself like Jean and would be lucky if I did get "discovered" in my seventies, which now didn't even seem that far away. I too was a writer that people like Oskar could not read. It was only other writers who liked my work. And why was that true of Jean and myself? We wrote baldly about the sadness of life, and not much else. Marguerite seemed to also take on that subject but her characters were often the ones doling out the sadness. In Jean's and my books, we received it and then I swung my mind back to Marta's recitations, and both Marguerite and Jean were intently listening to her, neither of them feeling the grief I was . . .

"Heidrich was the only Nazi official assassinated. And this happened in Prague," Marta said. "Of course the reprisals were pretty awful . . ."

Jean began humming: "*Bei mir bist du schön.*"

Marguerite and I looked at her as if she was mad.

She smiled and said, "Humming keeps me warmer. I like those Yiddish songs."

I smiled embarrassed, since; for one thing, I thought it was a jazz song, and certainly not one to bring up when Marta's countrymen had been murdered. On the other hand, isn't insisting on life the only response to any brutality?

"Didn't Benny Goodman record it?" I asked.

Both Marguerite and Jean said, "Everybody recorded it."

The three of us began walking again with our umbrellas. The blonde woman stayed out ahead of us.

"Why don't we," I said, "write a book about the Prague jewels, the three of us, and how the Czechs foil Heidrich. All around the keys. The seven characters." I turned my head toward Marguerite. "How many just men are there supposed to be in the world?"

"Thirty-six," Marguerite said. Thirty-six men born into the world each generation to save us from complete destruction. Or, let's say, from irrevocable destruction.

"In point of fact, I am sure there are not quite as many," Jean said, drily.

"The thirty-six just men are actually an Islamic and Persian lore, besides Jewish—" Marguerite said.

"Well anyway," I said, "one of the men could be one of the just men. One of the men who foil the Nazis."

Marguerite smiled at Jean. "At least she's thinking about just men . . . instead of an unloving one. It's a start."

I could see they were not interested in writing a book with me; they were too independent for that. And I didn't really want to write one with them either. But I loved sharing the idea of the Prague jewels being protected. I loved the idea of anything being protected.

I walked behind them lost in thought. So lost, I could have been anywhere, not here in Prague. I thought about my last night with Oskar, which was cold as always. Why would I insist on someone like that? I wondered.

Jean turned around and was smiling. She lifted her umbrella for me to catch up with them. I did catch up. "What are we doing this afternoon?" she asked.

"I think a monastery next," I said.

"Oh," she said, ignoring her own question and answering instead what I had been thinking about. "You're full of love, you know. You're not impaired. Wait and see what happens when the right one comes along. You'll give all, like everyone else who loves does."

I smiled painfully, as if what she inferred might not be true. "No doubt you haven't spent much time in monasteries," I said.

"No," she said. "Luckily, I haven't."

Marguerite changed her mind. Synagogues instead. Off we went to the Jewish quarter, where the streets are tiny and four Synagogues were practically lined up in a row. One Synagogue had all the artifacts of Jewish culture before the war. One gave out to a Jewish cemetery of ancient gravestones that sat like gaping grey teeth in the ground. One had a history of all the prestigious Czech Jews—Freud, Mahler and others. And one Synagogue had a list of everyone who had been shipped to Theresienstadt and Auschwitz inscribed on its walls.

I walked around, looking at all these names, and to entertain myself I looked up my mother's name, she was Jewish and European and I knew of course her family would be there but it was still different seeing them all named and I knew she had lost everyone as a child. They snuck her out to Palestine, these dead people, these alive names. I had told myself that out of loyalty to her family, my mother could not bond with me. Why should she have a loving life and not they? It was her way of honoring them, to reject me. But deep down I knew that was nonsense. She rejected me because that was who she was. Or worse, because that is who I am. Maybe I had forced her with my flagrant independence. At four, though? All I could remember now was my own unlovingness. How hurt I was and how I cowered away. She had always said I was timid in love. And I had been too timid to respond, And why wouldn't I be with the way you walked from me?

I kept walking and did not mention my theories to the two women.

That night we sat in an Italian restaurant for dinner, one that displayed a number of fish with their heads staring at us on a platter.

We were hungry after our day of sightseeing. We had gone to the monastery after all, once we had seen the synagogues. First the Jews, then the legendary Jewish martyr.

I still did not mention my family's names on the wall. It was not a surprise to me; it was just seeing them, the terrible sadness of it. Maybe that history was what had made me think what's the point of taking care of oneself. Fate deals with you as it will. Everything important is on the inside, the outside can't be trusted.

Let me talk about something else, anything else.

"The Czech republic is a country of atheists," I said, "so there aren't too many monks to come back here and take care of that monastery we saw today. The guide said they mostly come in from Poland and even then there aren't enough. Maybe there are only 11 monks in that huge monastery tending 200 acres of grounds, on top of the library, and . . ." Jean said, "Extraordinary."

Marguerite was eating soup. Then she stopped and just looked out the window.

And there it was again. All three of us were silent for a minute imagining the lives of these young men probably from poor devout families who now have the responsibility of this enormous wealth but are an anachronism in every way, having grown up with nothing and now tending the world's riches. All for the promise of inheriting the next world's riches.

"Of course writers are a dying out group too," Marguerite said.

"We are not dying out," I said. "Just there are no outlets for us. Luckily the internet will publish anyone. No matter how bad we are. Who knows who will read the stuff?"

Jean said, "Maybe some should become monks. It's a good life for a writer. Look at the Renaissance and what it produced."

"Well it certainly was beautiful there," I added. "Wouldn't it be nice to just sit there and write a book? For two months," I said.

"Certainly could improve the recruitment business for monks, telling them it'll turn them into writers," Marguerite said, ignoring me. "In my time, people didn't think everyone could do it. It was an intellectual's activity. Now it's for anyone who can use a keyboard."

"It's interesting, isn't it?" I said, thinking how much I could hate the world. What about all those brilliant people who wrote on concentration camp walls? What about their writing? No internet for them. Just a cry.

Then I remembered something from her book, *Emily L.*, again. "Do you remember this, Marguerite? You wrote it. '*Writing means, among other things, not knowing what you're doing, being unable to judge it—there's certainly a bit of that in writing, a blinding light. And then there's the fact that it takes up a great deal of time and calls for a lot of effort—that's an attraction too. It's one of the few occupations that never stops being interesting.*'"

"Doesn't sound that interesting when you recite it like that. But I did write it," Marguerite said. "You mean everyone wants to write now because they are bored? I don't know. Anyway, I could never be in a monastery writing. I always needed to be in love when I was writing a book."

Jean said, "Me too."

"Me too," I said. "But the monks were probably in love with each other."

"In fact," Marguerite added, "I never had any desire to BE in a monastery. You have to want to run away from sexual desire to join, I suppose. All the desire is for the perfect love of God.

I, on the other hand, loved sex, as you know. How demanding desire is. How you are powerless against it. A desire for tenderness that is almost violent. I miss it. Even . . . you know . . . where we are now."

I was wondering where they were now but decided time will tell, time will tell. In more ways than one, I rued.

"Well old age does that," Jean said. "Makes people run away from sex. From having it with you." And she laughed at her joke.

"It's not funny," Marguerite said. We all looked sadly at the handsome Italian waiters knowing we could not pull their interest any more.

"It is funny that talking about a monastery gets us to sex."

"Yes, get near any prohibition and woof . . . out come all the desires. That's what the guide said." And here Jean did an imitation of Marta, after all Jean had been an actress for quite some time. "This is what communism did," she said, in Marta's insistent heavy Czech accent. I watched Jean's luminous blue eyes vamp and I imagined her on the bare wooden stages round England, dancing, and singing. Afterwards going to her boarding house rooms, her eyes even more huge through the make up.

Marguerite smiled but I noticed she wasn't saying anything. I knew it was Jean's reference to Communism. Marguerite had been one, like all the French intellectuals. But, like Camus, she withdrew when she saw what Stalin had got up to. The Party threw her out. But she always claimed she was a Communist in her heart. She believed in man caring for man. Hah! That's a good joke.

"Communism has essentially ended, except in Cuba, so what does it all matter?" I said. "Like arguing the Roman government's edicts. So much for man's goodness to man."

Marguerite said, "Why would anyone write unless one believes in man's goodness to man? It's the only reason to write."

I nodded.

"True," I said, guiltily. "Anyway, the Czechs sure hated the Communists."

"Everybody hates an invader," Marguerite said. "Even if we do end up flirting with them."

"Or marrying them," Jean added.

When the fish was served, sans faces, we ate with a great passion, all three of us, and drank as if we were hearty marauders and, again, it was not that we spoke of any subject that was so marvelously enlightening. It was the being together that was enlightening. I felt loved and surrounded. I didn't feel alone. I felt, safe and untroubled, with people who accepted me and I, them.

I raised my second glass of wine. I had been alone it seemed all my life, frightened to trust men who said they loved me, frightened to take chances. Now that all seemed to be changing. I don't know why, everything was changing from not being so alone.

"Thank you so much," I said. "This is how it should always be."

"Well it won't be," Marguerite said, "so enjoy it now. And think up ways to have it like this in your own life. You should be traveling, talking, writing, sharing, seeing, laughing, being loved, loving . . ."

I didn't want to be so mundane as to ask how. Anyway I am sure that too was on the agenda.

I looked over at Jean and Marguerite with their faces that spoke of so much rebellion, insistence on being themselves, so much loss, and so much beauty on the page and perhaps even at times, with lovers and friends, and I thought, these, these are my ancestors. I was not unaware of the conceit of that, but I did believe if you ask, you will receive, and it must have been that brokenness in me, of writing that wasn't taking, of insistent independence, of feeling unworthy of love, and yet so desirous, so desirous, it was all so clamoring, that that was why, they came back.

NINE

Vienna was next. We three took a train, a four-hour train, and none of us looked out the window, only occasionally at the pristine open farmland between the two countries. What we did, instead, was read. All three of us completely involved in our respective books, with Jean nodding off a bit.

I interrupted Marguerite, "What are you reading?"

"Stendhal," she said. "This is a way of keeping me in touch with love. It makes me feel alive."

I looked over at what Jean was reading. Duras.

"She's made an interesting choice," I said to Marguerite.

"Which one is it?"

I leaned over to see. The book was on Jean's lap, as Jean slept. *The War*.

Marguerite grunted. "I can see she's engrossed."

"She's tired," I said.

"And you?" Marguerite asked. "What are you reading?"

"Pamuk's Norton Lectures on the novel."

"As if there are any rules."

"There are millions of writing schools now, you know," I said, to be provocative.

"Idiotic. In my day writing was about individualism. Not commercialism."

"Well . . ." I didn't want to say that day had passed. "The good stuff still wins out."

She sighed and said, "I would hope so."

When we got to Vienna, we checked into where they had booked us, The Hotel Sacher, another gorgeous hotel. I could not believe the opulence. Such a gift. They both were very unconcerned about the bill. I don't know if I have ever been unconcerned about a bill.

"Did we pay the hotel in Prague? I didn't, I know that," I said. "I wouldn't be able to."

"I paid it," Marguerite said.

"How?" I asked.

"I used a credit card. In the States, they give a credit card to anyone, even a dead person. So I used it."

I laughed.

"I remember a writer telling me," Marguerite said, "that a writer should always accept money."

"Really?"

"Yes," she said, pedagogically.

After checking in, we three walked a little round the hotel and oohed and aahed at the blue bar, the velvet couches, the marble walls, the beautiful wood floors with plush red carpets. We looked across the street and we found ourselves facing the enormous Wiener Staatsoper, Opera House that Marguerite says is not so amazing inside because it was bombed in the war, and the rebuilding in the 1950s is the height of mediocrity with square, small rooms without windows.

"Why did you want to come back here?" I asked her.

"At this point," she said, "I am happy anywhere."

We were all taken with the grandness of the opera's exterior and could imagine the imperialness of the opera conductors who were the kings of that house. And thus the kings of Vienna. Mahler, Von Karajan, Strauss.

Then I decided to take them to the Weiner Philharmoniker. We walked along the Ringstrasse, past the regal hotels and handsome stone, elegant buildings that spoke to me of witty meetings with brilliant Austrian journalists out-ironicizing each other over politics, love and writing; elegant buildings that seemed to conjure up beautifully dressed women with cream skin, not harshly sophisticated like French women, but feminine and wise similar to . . . I wasn't sure, Hedy Lamarr? My dead mother? My dead grandmother? And wasn't Marie Antoinette in effect Austrian? We continued walking past more of these stately handsome buildings that could also, with another eye, appear harbingers of coldness, housing tall elegant Austrian men deaf to the cries of Jews or Gypsies or gays or *mischlings* and then we came to the Musikverein, another stolid stone building, with elegant lit windows that made the building seem like it was wearing silver and gold.

I am used to Carnegie Hall, which at first seemed to me to be more opulent but, as I settled into my seat, I thought maybe I am wrong. The seats are not as plush as Carnegie Hall but the gold sculptures, the strength in that symphony hall, the fact that Beethoven and everyone else had been played here for centuries to perfection, overcame me.

We got our seats and I noticed the orchestra sat closer to the audience than in America. I felt I was back in another day, looking at orchestras of ancient renown and then I realized why: the orchestra was all men. No dainty Asian girls with their violins. No stalwart East European women with dyed hair and their cellos. Just the calling up of powerful music, in the powerful hands of men. Politically incorrect as it was, there was something thrilling about it, men playing their hearts out for us.

"Like it was in my time," Jean said. I turned to look at her sitting elegantly in her pink orange silk dress, and then I turned to Marguerite dressed up in black satin pants and an Indochine silk black jacket with the Nehru collar. They both looked lovely.

I could see they were thrilled to be here. The orchestra first played some Wagner. Okay. Beautiful.

There was one man. An oboist near the back of the orchestra. Longish grey hair. Tall, lanky, a sensitive face. Intense. A touch removed.

I stared at him the entire Bruckner. He had a perfect oval face that when I tried to imagine it young, struck me as maybe being too handsome, too perfect. I liked the cragginess of it now that he was in his sixties. I liked his intensity on his instrument. I liked that he was serious. I liked that he had enormous delicate hands. I liked that I was liking someone.

"He's my type," I whispered to Marguerite.

She pointed to a more kempt, paunchier man, he could have been a businessman, or a man who would be nice to you. He was forcefully playing his violin, like a *burgher*, bourgeoisie, in a small French town. "My type," she said.

She obviously went for men who could possibly give her something.

Jean was peering around at the people around us. "Very nice jewelry," she said, looking at the rapt Viennese women. Then she turned to me, "What are you looking at?"

I leaned in. "If you are capable of coming back to life . . ."

"Yes?"

"Introduce me to that oboist and make sure I spend the rest of my life with him."

She put her glasses on and studied him. Bruckner's *Allegro* was pouring out of the Philharmonik. They were playing their instruments with a fury. I felt inexorably happy. Jean sighed.

"What?" I said, even though the music was wonderfully drowning me out.

"It's breathtaking, isn't it," she whispered. "The absolute exquisiteness of it." The music was filling the entire hall, a pitch where all our souls were vibrating. She leaned in, "I remember Madox Ford saying if you want to be a novelist you must first be a poet and it is impossible to be a poet and lack human sympathies or generosity of outlook." She leaned in closer, "Music embraces all of that."

"True," I whispered back.

Then she leaned into me and whispered, "Alright."

"Alright what?" I asked while glancing over at Marguerite. She was listening intently but I had the feeling the music was not affecting her as much as it did Jean and me. Music for her probably was about film. How to integrate the images. She was deeply focused and I had the thought she was running a film in her own mind. I did not think she was running old films that she had written and directed. I thought she was making one right then as she blindly listened and watched the Philharmonik.

"I'll introduce you to the oboist," Jean whispered.

TEN

We had agreed to meet for breakfast the next day in the marble breakfast room with its row of white orchids along the ledge with one matching flower languishing on each table. Men in white tails bowed while quietly pouring coffee into one's delicate white china cup, just as the thought of coffee flitted across one's mind.

We had agreed to meet there, but none of us showed up. Instead, we each called each other's room and said we wanted to do some writing.

I couldn't imagine what writing again would be like for both of them. For one thing, they didn't know computers. Jean, I could see in my mind's eye, delicate and serious, sitting at the Hotel Sacher mahogany desk, ordering in coffee, beginning slowly and surely, and absolutely perfectly, with a pencil, writing her story about a woman lost on these Viennese *strasses*. Her lead character's coat not warm enough, but still attractive, denoting pride. That dastardly pride that makes you sink, since you can't ask anyone to help you. You refuse to believe you can't take care of yourself. "It will be better tomorrow."

Her character would meet some Viennese cad, who would give her warmth, and maybe a few Euros, enough to get through the night so to speak but, of course, shortly she would be left alone.

Marguerite must be sitting down also, with focus, her big glasses on, but she would have insisted someone find her a typewriter. And they would have found it. This is an old world here. And French women insist well.

As she began, she would perhaps be more affected by Vienna itself and imagining how the Anschluss speech took place right near the hotel in the Holstein Palace gardens. Or how yesterday she had thrown her earphones down in the Jewish Museum when they had displayed what she called lies, Mahler as a great Viennese Jew.

"He was a Bohemian Jew, for one thing," she said, "and he had to become a Christian to conduct here. What kind of great Viennese Jew is that? I'm leaving . . ."

Jean said, "Good idea," because she found all this philo-Semitism tiring. "It is a Jewish preoccupation," she said, "to be preoccupied with being a Jew since it is part of their religion, but, let's face it, it is wearing for the rest of us."

All my British relatives had felt the same way about the subject. They also felt my Jewish mother was a touch wearing, to say the least. On this topic, I would have to agree. She had a tendency to only speak of herself. And it was wearing trying to hide, from her and myself, my broken, clamoring self.

Anyway Marguerite might be taking Vienna's historical miskeys for her story. She tended to write more with anger. Jean with defeat. Both were lamenting love. One strictly in a personal story, the other maybe through a political story. Although, it is of note, that Marguerite's real success came through a personal story.

I looked at my laptop. What should I write about? My real life was more fanciful than anything I could think up. Maybe that had always been the problem. I had written stories and novels (some were published and most were not) about my life that were true, about a girl all alone, braving the elements, a girl who flirted with her mother's boyfriends to get her mother's attention, and still was not able to; a woman who had trouble feeling. The editors' unanimous responses were, "Couldn't happen." I wish.

I went to my email, the biggest distraction ever invented for writers, beating out infidelity, mirror gazing and the telephone. It has all the seduction (you are writing; you are not alone but no one is bothering you) but none of the real feeling.

I saw an email from my current freelance employer. Her email said she could not pay me anymore. It was true there was nothing more for me to do for her and we both knew it. I had other irons in the fire, they just weren't hot, in fact they seemed to be made of that kind of iron that never acquires heat.

I was so beaten down by this news, more money problems, did they never end? That I couldn't even be bothered to tell Jean and Marguerite. I played some jazz on the hotel CD player and thought about these men, these jazz musicians, and the continual struggle—and music—of their lives and I felt some relief from my own problems. Is it the struggle or the isolation of the struggle that is hard to bear? I was not sure.

When I got back to the States, I decided, I would try and find something else. As always. I was well aware that when you live on the outside of society, it gets harder and harder.

But the fact is that my rent is more than the rent of two houses in Des Moines, my health insurance more than 5 houses in Africa and my income as stable as investing in buggy whips.

I walked around the hotel room. I looked at myself in the bathroom mirror. Yes, it was I. At least that person never seemed to abandon me. Back to the desk.

The Prague jewels. God, aren't we all sick of Nazi stories by now? The writers who have made careers out of the Second World War. What would fiction have done without the Second World War?

The Strahov Monastery. Too quiet for me and I didn't want to spend a year in the minds of monks. And the research, good god. It would not, shall we say, come naturally to me.

I looked outside the window at the Opera House. I had already written about Mahler. I was through with him, too.

So I began. A woman. Older. Broke. Alone, as David Markson had written so nakedly about himself, in one of his books, aptly named *The Last Novel*. Back to my story. My character would be a dreamer. She's a jazz musician without skill on her instrument. Depends who's listening. Alright, skill, I'll give her some skill. I don't need to be so rough on her. She gave her life to music and men. When she did play, she played well. She was naturally adventurous and played in her own style. Some liked it, some didn't. She couldn't adhere to others' style and this was, to her, the mark of being a true artist. She just didn't plan on a life alone, but maybe unconsciously she had—she had. She had thought the right man, a serious one, a loving one, would come along. Maybe he had and she had mistreated him.

Now my character had to come up with something or it was death. She had to resolve all this. You can't change aging. That she had to surrender to. It was too late for her to start a new career. Maybe too late to meet the Prince who would help her. And so she...

She could go on the internet and find some old cat but no, I'd have to write too many disappointing characters. Anyway she liked believing in the creativity of fate, even if it did have a tendency to be a bit unkind. But there's always a surprise. Across a crowded room and all. Why not? Fate changes in an instant. Hers needed to.

I turned away from the P.C. I myself didn't know how to vanquish the obstacles so how could I make my character do so? Could these women teach me? That I even wanted teachers was a sign of new health on my part.

Marguerite and Jean had had enormous talent, and they waited the long haul for their ships to come in. A helluva wait when you thought about it. Jean waited till into her late seventies, as you know. Somebody working at the BBC did a radio play of one of her earlier, out-of-print books and that began Jean's revivification. The producer put a call out in certain magazines. Does anyone know the whereabouts of Jean Rhys? Jean was living broke in some small British town. From then on, Deutsch Publishers brought her out with that marvelous editor, Diana Athill, who took her on, understood her, and the editor herself became a stunning writer in her seventies, eighties and nineties, about being in your seventies, eighties and nineties. Jean once said when she was alive, that writing was like an ocean. Tolstoy was a major river flowing in. But she, Jean, was a small tributary contributing to the sea. It turned out her editor too contributed to the sea. We're all contributing to that sea. Given how much people are writing on the internet, it would seem that sea is going to get clogged up.

Marguerite, in her sixties, finally told the truth about her shame, usurousness, the price she paid for being used. How the young girl in her story was sold to a rich Chinese lover and the rest of her life bore a hopelessness that she sublimated into an intense, vigorous, successful life of writing. That novel, in fact, all her novels are inextricably sad, elegiac, resonating string quartets as told through her fierce eyes.

I suddenly thought about close friends of mine in their seventies going to funerals.

I switched to my email.

A film producer with no money talking to a co-producer who also has no money. They forwarded me an email between them. One had written, "Very few have the ability of Mira who doesn't destroy or mock but rather gives us a magical gift."

Even I, flattering as it was, had to ask myself what the hell was he talking about. Frankly, I didn't know but it was a wonderful email to receive anyway. But he didn't have any money to make a film. Talk as art. Talk as talking about art.

I thought about the date I had been fixed up with a month ago, another attempt on my part to topple Oskar's reign in my life. A friend set me up with a successful novelist who gets a million dollars for his books and he had told me on the phone how much he admires Jean Rhys and Duras and Richard Yates and Graham Greene. The successful novelist had just signed a movie deal for enormous money, he told me, as we sipped Old Fashioned's together. The movie deal would help support the houses he owns in Berlin, Paris, London and Maine. He had been knighted by the French. He was tall, smart and sexy and, earlier in the evening; he had suggested we go hear a French pianist, a man who wrote the music to *Breathless*. While the pianist played (a little too intellectually, I thought) I smiled at my date, at a particularly lovely transition in the music. My date, in response, took my hand. We had only known each other ten minutes. What is he doing, I wondered. He continued holding and fondling my hand. I thought, Okay. Let's see what this is all about.

After the music, we decided to have a drink to get to know each other. We were walking in the late night and he stopped in the middle of the street to kiss me. It seemed I was under attack by an invading army. So far not an interesting one, yet what invasion is interesting?

We made pleasant conversation at the bar although the fact he didn't like his parents or his ex-wife or his siblings was what another woman I know refers to as "pink flags."

"Do you want to see my hotel room?" he asked.

I thought, We'll continue talking without getting drunk.

Clearly he thought, I'll get laid.

When I didn't want to sleep with him, having only known him two hours at this point, he got ice cold.

Success doesn't always bring the best out in people.

But the broke producer's compliment about my writing did inspire me and that was what I had to sustain myself on right now. That one sentence.

I would have to live on that sentence to create sentences, as Jean and Marguerite were both creating sentences in their hotel rooms. Creating sentences as manifest destiny that they are alive. And why not?

Rather than think about my own sentences, I went on to think about seeing Oskar the next night after my abortive date with the successful novelist. Oskar thought the story funny. "You'll never be able to replace me," he said. "I am perfect for you. You need my distance. It inspires you. You would destroy us if we got closer."

"You realize that's insulting?" I said, sitting on what he calls "my perch" by the fire.

He shrugged. He didn't see what was insulting about it. He never saw how his projections were insulting.

I went back to my story about the jazz musician. Jean no doubt was on her English woman runaway in Vienna. Some remake of what she had written in *Quartet* because we're always writing the same book. "*Love was a terrible thing. You poisoned it and stabbed at it and knocked it down into the mud—well down—and it got up and staggered on, bleeding and muddy and awful. Like—like Rasputin . . .*"

Last night Jean said at dinner, "Looking back on my life, I see that the only solid thing has been my writing."

Marguerite, in response, had a little smile on her face. "I am going to do something that will cheer you up," she said, taking a bite of her ravioli. She particularly enjoyed the food, of being alive. Jean, on the other hand, hardly noticed it. But she did notice the scotch.

What does go on after you die? I wondered. It wasn't that far away.

"What?" I asked.

"I am going to be so gauche as to quote your old pal," she said to me. And she laughed, and then we began to laugh at her laughing because it was wonderful to see her joyful. And of course, *Emily L.*, at this point, was almost a friend. Marguerite began. "*And I said one ought to write without making corrections, not necessarily at full tilt, no, but at one's own pace and in accordance with what one is experiencing at the time; one ought to eject what one writes, manhandle it almost, yes, treat it roughly, not try to trim profusion but let it be part of the whole, and not tone down anything either, whether its speed or its slowness, just leave everything as it is when it appears.*"

Not a bad idea.

So now Marguerite was probably in her room writing about a woman knowing the world has gone mad, and finding a man to make love to who is neither German, Austrian, French nor European. He is the Other. Not particularly safe either, she would find out, because love isn't safe. But her character would find some unsafe means of finding Safety. Her character would find it through loving the Other. And then, through that, the world.

And so in that Hotel Sacher, which felt like a ship, all three of our minds that morning, were steadily moving onto the paper in front of us.

ELEVEN

We were walking through a piazza near the hotel looking for a bookstore when we saw a man in a hat and coat standing by one of the Baroque fountains full of angels. He was looking about like he was being followed.

"Must be the Third Man," I joked.

"No," Marguerite said. "It's not."

"Look at the color of his pants, they're almost yellow," Jean said.

I peered more closely. Only one man dresses like that.

Oh my god. It was. Oskar.

My heart soared; he had come to meet me. He does care for me.

Till he began smiling and raising his arm, to another woman. A younger woman, coming toward him in a brocade jacket and pants. She had red hair cut in a pageboy. My heart soared alright, downward.

They both looked at me sadly. Jean said, "I'm sorry. It happens to all of us as we get older."

I was too hurt to speak. All I saw as my eyes frantically travelled up and down the street was a gold plaque on the building behind where my two companions were standing. It's some kind of office building. Let me go hide in there.

"I, I have to be alone right now," I said.

And before they could respond, I flew into what turned out to be a doctors' building. Up the elevator to where the door opened to a brisk Austrian nurse.

Didn't bother me at all. I was ill alright.

And this particular doctor turned out to be a plastic surgeon.

I felt a bit guilty abandoning the women so abruptly like that but there are times, as Charles Bukowski said, that are best to stay away from other writers and just do your work, or just not do your work.

"May I help you," the blonde, sharp-eyed nurse said with a polite clippedness.

I did not quite know what to do. "I, I don't have an appointment. I—"

"That's alright, we just had a cancellation, follow me," and the white-soled shoes firmly turned down a hallway. I followed her, hoping maybe he would kill me.

Then I was in a small room with one of those chairs that you can lie down in and a tall bald handsome Austrian man in a white coat was peering down at me exceptionally closely. "You need a face lift. Your cheek is falling in here."

I didn't even want to look at it.

"I could puff up your lips," he said. "This would give you a younger look."

"Do it."

He began painfully putting needles in my lips. Never mind people had always told me I had good lips. I hated myself right now.

The pain didn't faze me at all. I felt much worse inside.

"Put this ice on your lips to help with the swelling."

I sat there with the ice, tears forming. He thought it was from the pain of the shots, but I was quite aware what it was really from. Some part of me felt Oskar would become my mate, reality notwithstanding. Well, another delusion stinging me in the face. Pass the needle.

"Actually," the cold surgeon said, "I could stave off the face lift by putting a filler in your cheeks."

"Do it," I said.

I cursorily checked for a charge card. I had one.

He began shooting something into my face. It hurt. He seemed to be enjoying himself. Had I found the last Nazi doctor?

"One moment," he said and went off to get more of his solution or maybe a longer needle. It didn't matter to me. I lay there in pain looking up at his ceiling, waiting. I thought about how Jean had written about this in one of her books. "*Loving had done that to her—among other things—made her ugly. This was love—this perpetual aching longing, this wound that bled persistently and very slowly, and the devouring hope. And the fear. That was the worst. The fear she lived with—that the little she had would be taken from her.*"

The doctor returned, went back into my cheeks, and finally he was finished.

"More ice," he said.

I looked in the mirror. I pulled back. What I saw was a complete lookalike for Miss Piggy. Big lips that were not the shape of my lips at all. Big floppy lips, those fake lips that you see on dastardly old women trying to look young, those women whose eyes look back at you fearfully as you look at them even more fearfully, fearing you will be one of them yourself. And now I am. My cheeks stuck out like torpedo bombs, about to be activated. I could not have looked more horrible. Or more unnatural.

"It's swelling," he said. "It will go down."

Now look what I've done. I've ruined my face and now that I thought about it, I had a pretty face to begin with. I had known that deep down. Why did I forget? Now I was a monster on top of everything else.

My insides now matched my outsides.

I paid too much money. I felt sick from the swelling and sick when I looked in the mirror and sick at Oskar's not loving me.

Now he and I were even: I couldn't love me either.

TWELVE

Marguerite had drawn the curtains open before I got there, the result being that the light coming into the room cast an unambiguous accuracy to the distorted contours of my face.

"It doesn't look that bad," Marguerite said, but I was pretty sure she was understating.

"Well now no one will ever love me," I said. "Or at least not for 6 months they won't."

"Yes, you're right, it's not permanent," Jean said. "Try not to look in the mirror," she added. She could see I kept checking to see if I was coming back to my real self.

"It feels worse," Marguerite said, "because you feel the swelling. It can only go down."

"Thank you," I said, "for not expounding on my being an idiot."

They said nothing, and shifted their bodies as they sat on their beds, out of nervousness, a nervousness in beginning to remember all the insecurities, stupidities, vagrancies of being alive.

"I will tell you however," Marguerite said sternly, "that you're impulsive."

I nodded.

"I should have remembered what you wrote in *The Lover*. Why didn't I remember that?" I said.

"What?" she asked, once again impatiently. I think she didn't like her books being referred to constantly.

"*One day, I was already old, in the entrance of a public place a man came up to me. He introduced himself and said; 'I've known you for years. Everyone says you were beautiful when you were young, but I want to tell you I think you're more beautiful now than then. Rather than your face as a young woman, I prefer your face as it is now. Ravaged.'"*

Jean said, "Wonderful, Marguerite. Beautiful."

Marguerite said, "But, in deference to her," she said looking at me, "most people do prefer ravishing to ravaged."

"Well, we're all ravaged now," said Jean. "At least in the form we've come back in."

"Odd, isn't it?" I said. "I wonder why you came back as you were at the end."

"Maybe we were at our best then," Jean answered. "As Marguerite was writing."

"Oh come on," Marguerite said, "I would much rather have come back sexually attractive. It's ridiculous we came back this way. I mean," she continued, "it's good for her, we appear like kind old ladies, but really, Jean, wouldn't you like to buy some decent clothes and walk in a room and be the center of attention? Have everyone notice and desire us?"

"At least until they've had us," Jean said.

"Those moments are everything," Marguerite continued rapturously. "Who cares that they're only moments? They add up."

"Well, you are at your best in lots of ways," I said. "I'm sorry you're not young. I'm sorry I myself am not young.

Or I wouldn't have done this . . . (I pointed to my face). Anyway we should keep sightseeing." I did not want to ruin their trip. "What are we doing tonight?" I said, catching the bruising on my face as I took another peak in the mirror, hoping the swelling would just magically disappear. I looked ridiculous with two enormous cheeks and distended lips.

"The thing is," Jean said, sitting up, "you're busy tonight."

"What do you mean?"

"I arranged that you meet Mr. Vienna, the oboist from the Philharmonik. I introduced myself to him this morning during his rehearsals and told him he should meet my niece. He thought it was an amusing idea, and actually he, unlike most people, HAD read my books so of course he was thrilled to join you, me, although he had not read about my life obviously or he would have known I am dead. But in a way I prefer when they know your work and not your life. I can't stand the constant comparisons. Which is the better story? Your life or your work? Obviously, it's the work. Who the hell can make a neat ending to a life? He will be in the lobby at 7."

"What will I do with my face?"

"You have to go anyway," Marguerite said, standing up and rearranging her hairbrush and creams on her side table. "He doesn't know your real face."

"He will think I'm a grotesque."

"It's not THAT bad. It's just not the you we know. But he doesn't know that you. You have to keep moving on."

"I'm going to go lie down in my room," I said, "and cry."

"Good idea," Jean said, also standing up, suddenly agitated. Life, I could see her thinking, is so full of these strange transitory preoccupations . . . "I'll order up some arnica to put on it. And then you must go out tonight."

They both had expressions of frustration on their faces. Was it remembering this business of thinking one is not good enough for a man because one knows a man is inspired by some inner romance with beauty, as a salve to his own wounds? Were they remembering how men's eyes lingered on their young bodies? The endless compliments? How that mesmerization might not have been so wholesome, it was not your well-being these men were considering, or many of them, and then the human activity of men, men like Oskar, who did not want to know the woman but only enough to make him feel marvelous about himself. As Virginia Woolf said, men want you to mirror them back three times their size. Not all men, I admit. There are good ones. But those aren't the ones who do this ravaging of you that ends up with your ravaging yourself.

"Don't let this overwhelm you so," Marguerite said. "You are more than just a pretty face. Or not pretty face. You are who you are inside. Maybe this is what you needed to learn."

"The hard way," I said.

"Is there any other?" Jean asked. "Seven in the lobby."

I nodded and picked up my handbag slowly, stood up and shuffled to the door.

THIRTEEN

The Weiner Philharmoniker oboist stood waiting by a huge basket of red flowers in the Hotel Sacher lobby. The subdued light (thank god) set off his dark, grey hair, his blue jacket, grey sweater. He looked like he was from a film, tall, elegant, waiting to take you into a drawing room and from then on in you would be eternally happy. Miss Sunset Boulevard meet Mr. Viennese Rhett Butler.

He put out his long fingered hand and smiled into my eyes, which I consoled myself at that moment had not been fiddled with. Neither my small nose. Courage, I said to myself.

"Gerhardt," he said, extending his hand.

"Mira," I answered. And then those fingers full of music shook mine.

"Would you like a drink in the bar?" he asked. "It's quite cold out."

"I would love it. Maybe Jean and Marguerite will be there," I added.

"I don't think so," he said, as if he knew.

He took my elbow, seemingly unbothered that he was walking a distorted face through the hotel lobby. When we reached the bar, we sat down on the blue velvet couches and he ordered a scotch and I did the same.

"You must have been surprised," I smiled, my cheeks enormously full and painful, "at Jean's introduction. Do women often come up to you and ask you to meet their friends? Actually, to look at you, I would say yes."

"I was surprised," he said, leaning forward to grab some nuts. "I was surprised because I love her works. The film of *Wide Sargasso Sea* was not at all as good as her book. She is harsh with her characters, they cannot be happy, and certainly she portrays men as sources of torture, but all of it, all of it comes off as inevitably true. No?"

Men as sources of torture. "Yes," I said. But I could not help but notice that he was not avoiding me in conversation, as Oskar would do. Not to mention, one could also not avoid being a bit overcome by his long legs, his accent and sure voice, his seeming honesty. Why did I do this? My face felt like it kept growing as I sat there. It could come off my head any minute.

"Red is a lovely color for you," he said, generously.

I smiled back, although I felt defeated by everything.

"How long have you played with the Weiner Philharmoniker? It is such an orchestra. The force. The New York Phiharmonic is wonderful but there was something about the power of your . . ."

"Thirty years," he said. "I've been with them thirty years."

"You worked with Von Karajan?" I asked.

"Yes."

I wanted to just lie down and sleep next to him, knowing simply that.

"Do you like Russian choral singing?" I asked.

He looked surprised at the question. It's true; the question was a complete non sequitur. "Yes," he answered, "I do."

Of course he does. He's a musician. He likes music.

"Before we came to Europe, I went to a Russian chorus in the West Village," I said. "I sat by myself. Songs from *Peter the Great*. Rachmaninoff. It sort of restored me."

He nodded.

"Some trumpets, trombones," I said, reaching for conversation. "No oboes."

"No."

He decided to bring some sanity to the table. "Are you liking Vienna?"

"Vienna is a bit formal," I said, "with its empirical buildings, its neat Ringstrasse streets. But I feel one could take ten years to even begin to know what is going on behind these sound, lovely buildings. But of course it takes years to understand any city."

"Or any person," he added.

I turned to look at Gerhardt and the smoothness of his face almost hurt me and his head was cocked a little, as if he was listening to something . . .

"What is it?" I finally asked.

"The violin," he laughed, motioning to the music being piped in.

"Beethoven, I think."

He smiled, non-committal. At least, I thought it was Beethoven.

Then I heard discordance, or rather, I saw Oskar strolling into the bar. God, how this all hurt. He seemed to almost be the only presence.

I remembered a line from *Emily L.* again. I seem to be assailed by them. "*I don't know if love's a feeling. Sometimes I think it's a matter of seeing. Seeing you.*"

Oskar sat down with us, as if we had invited him. Which was bizarre. Just came and sat down and then I realized Oskar may be under some strange illusion that I am still his girlfriend, even though he seems to act as if he does not have the responsibilities or the desire of a boyfriend. He was dressed nattily as usual in a check jacket, as if he was out hunting which indeed he probably was.

What on earth is he doing here? He's supposed to be in New York. I am supposed to be starting a new life with new cheeks. Why is he here not letting me go toward a new life? Why does he think I deserve so little from him?

"Oskar, meet Gerhardt." They shook hands. Gerhardt smiled intelligently, confident I was with him.

At least his manner was confident.

"Where is your red-haired friend?" I asked Oskar.

"What red-haired friend?" he responded, smiling. He likes a contretemps.

"The one you were with today."

He looked a bit embarrassed for a minute. Then I quoted Jean who knew cads. "*He disliked being questioned and, when closely pressed, he lied. Not plausibly or craftily, but impatiently and absent-mindedly. So Maryha had long ago stopped questioning. For she was reckless, lazy, a vagabond by nature, and for the first time in her life she was very near to being happy.'"*

"What is that from?" he asked.

Gerhardt answered, "From *Quartet.*"

Oskar looked annoyed that someone knew something he didn't. He said, "I thought you women were a trio."

Then he looked at Gerhardt. "Or maybe you have become a quartet."

I didn't bother to respond.

"What have you done to your face?" he suddenly said, looking at me.

I shook my head. "A disaster. Don't ask."

"You didn't need to do anything to your face," he added. "There was nothing wrong with it."

Gerhardt said, "The allergic reaction will go down."

"Allergic reaction to what?" Oskar asked.

To you, I thought, although damnably I still found him attractive. Why did I find him attractive, this man who seemed to like me as an escort service? His activities I did not know about but suspected. Was I this malleable to him because of his electricity, or worse, his rejection?

"Allergic reaction to being emotionally alone," I answered. I looked at Gerhardt, "Present company excluded."

"I'm here, aren't I?" he shot back.

"I don't know why," I answered. "Oh yes, to meet her."

Gerhardt coughed.

"Gerhardt and I were just listening to music. What do you hear?" I asked Oskar.

"Mahler's hammer," he said smiling.

"Are you lovers?" Gerhardt asked.

"Were," I said.

"You always were volatile," Oskar said.

I debated debating with him.

"Good," Gerhardt said and took my hand. "Because, Oskar, we are off to dinner—I hope you are enjoying your stay in our historic city."

"Morally historically reprehensible," Oskar said, annoyed. Oskar is Jewish. He should go talk to Marguerite.

Gerhard stood up taller than Oskar. I stood up too.

"I can't be toyed with anymore," I said to Oskar.

"What do you mean? I came here to see you."

I shook my head in confusion.

Gerhardt gently put his hand on the small of my back. "We must go, Oskar. A pleasure to meet you. By the way," he said, "that is a very excellent jacket you are wearing."

And even though Oskar had no idea what was going on, we left him there cottoning to the compliment.

FOURTEEN

When I came down to breakfast in the hotel dining room, the next morning, Marguerite and Jean were there, but also seated was a small, older man. He had sharp dark eyes, and he seemed to be speaking quickly. He must be French, I thought. He was very busy explaining something.

I came and sat down with them. "Hello," Marguerite said, her eyes gay, quite delighted in fact. "This is our friend Mira," she said to him. "André."

"Bonjour," I said. He smiled charmingly at me, assessing me as men do, so unabashedly. I now wonder how I register in their assessments, whereas thirty years ago I did not have to wonder.

"I knew André as a child in Saigon. Isn't that strange? We used to take walks together. My mother would not let me talk to him too much so we wrote letters," Marguerite said.

Jean added in, "You were involved in erotographomania."

"What?" Marguerite said.

"Nobody uses that word anymore," I said and then turned to Marguerite. "Love letters. It means love letters."

I looked back at Jean who was watching Marguerite and André rather curiously, as if to gauge whether this could really happen.

"How did you two find each other?" I asked.

"André is staying here too and he is in Vienna doing business. Isn't that amazing?"

I noticed Marguerite had undone one of her sweater buttons so you could see her cleavage slightly. That heavy cleavage of older women. Would he like it? I wondered. He seemed rather entranced sitting there. These women, let's face it, had, if not young skin, gravitas. That must count for something.

No one asked about my date.

André and Marguerite now began speaking in French and mostly about "Vienne," and also about going out tonight.

I had my sixth coffee, and finally said to Jean who was buttering her toast very intently, "By the way, I had the most marvelous time last night. I felt so relaxed and happy. Like I was myself. I could tell him anything."

"Really?" Marguerite asked, as if listening to both conversations.

"Gerhardt would say, 'Finish your sentence.' As if he wanted to know . . ."

"Well why shouldn't you like him?" Jean laughed. "He's talented, he's handsome, and . . . it sounds as if he's kind."

André asked if we were speaking about a priest.

I laughed. "No, *un musicien*."

"They're usually a bit abstract . . . self-absorbed," André said.

"That will come out later, I am sure," I replied.

Then I said to André, "Do you know this quote from" and here I nodded my head at Marguerite.

"Go on," he said.

"*You didn't have to attract desire. Either it was in the woman who aroused it or it didn't exist. Either it was there at first glance or else it had never been. It was instant knowledge of sexual relation-ship or it was nothing. That too I knew before I experienced it.'*"

Marguerite smirked. "I don't know what I was thinking writing that. I wrote as if I knew everything. And I knew nothing. Perhaps why everyone wants to write. While you're doing it, you feel like you know something which quickly evaporates when you're actually living life."

"True," both Jean and I said.

"Who were you writing about?" he asked Marguerite.

"How could I possibly remember?" she answered. Then she turned suspiciously to me, "How do you know if Gerhardt is taken with you?"

Jean said, "Why wouldn't he be?"

"Actually I saw him," Marguerite said. "I am not that impressed."

We all looked up, a bit surprised. She continued, "He does not have Oskar's style nor his outrageousness, which is a type of wit, and let us also keep in mind," she said in French fashion, "he has only an artist's money. We should not be so quick to dispense with Oskar."

"Oskar is cold," Jean said.

"So what?" Marguerite said. "Men are attractive in different ways. He makes her laugh. He's got class, well educated. Not to mention, why should she fall in love with a man in another city and one who can't offer her much security?"

André began to laugh.

"What is it?" she asked.

"You are worried about her falling in love with a man in another city? What about me falling in love with a woman in another time period?"

"We all must take chances in love," she said softly. "This is what it is."

It seems in their own particular cases, chances were alright. They're beyond chances. But they weren't the type not to take chances now . . . or then.

"Oskar offers her," Jean said, "absolutely nothing. Some patronizing conversation. I hardly think it is anything for her to hold onto."

Marguerite said nothing in return. Now they were a bit annoyed with each other.

"I don't know," I said, channeling my inner UN peacekeeping troops.

"Gerhardt acted as if he is capable of being in a relationship. But maybe he just behaves incredibly admirably with everyone. He has the same enthusiasm for life that I do. It turns out enthusiasm is sexy."

Marguerite looked at André.

I looked at Jean.

Jean looked at her tea.

Enthusiasm is sexy. Talent is sexy. Making art is sexy. Thinking is sexy. Living is sexy. Being is sexy.

That was when I took a few moments in my mind to replay last night. Gerhardt and I had been in a *kaffeehaus*, God knows which one. I had a café latte and berries *Mit Schlag*. He had some *Baba au rhum* that I uncharacteristically did not put my fork into, only because they had given me so much whipped cream with my own order that I was fully occupied and not having to scavenge.

"So you have no children either?" he asked.

"No. I decided not to."

Gerhardt was a tall, big man. He nodded and there was so much of him to listen to me. It was comforting.

"And you? Why did you not?" I asked him.

"My father was one of those Austrian burghers who believed in discipline. My mother was weak, actually strong in that she took care of us, but weak in that she could not handle him, and I did not want to re-experience all the feelings of childhood. Anyway, I had my music and music is very demanding."

"Anger," I said to the marble table.

"What do you mean?" he shot back.

Ah, anger is a hot button for him.

"Anger that we were hurt," I said softly. "That is why we had no children. We turned it inward."

Quite a psychological conversation for a first date. Must be something to do with the air in Freud's town.

"But I don't regret not having children," he said. "I wanted to be an artist. I knew I would have to have different priorities with children."

I sipped my coffee. I did regret it. Any turning away from love is regrettable.

"Anyway," he said, stabbing at his *Baba au rhum*, "I am a work in progress."

"What?"

"Women—you know, all of it—"

"A work in progress," I said smiling. "It's an American expression. But," I continued, "it's a beautiful thing to say." To me, it was a marvelous, humble, strong statement for a late middle-aged man to say, that he was a work in progress. It meant he was not full of himself. He did not think he was marvelous like certain other people we know. Then I began to wonder what he meant.

"A work in progress about women?" I repeated.

He smiled at me. "That's for another time."

"Okay," I answered. The young me would have insisted, Now, now, I want to know everything now. But I don't anymore. I trust that life will unfold. Everything gets revealed in the end and I don't believe what anyone says about themselves anyway.

My mind returned back to the breakfast room and its orchids and white china and Jean and Marguerite and now André. I took in his alert masculinity. He had nice lips. A gentle face. A good foil for Marguerite's fury. I hoped he would make love with her. But what Frenchman engages in a conversation with a woman he doesn't plan on sleeping with?

I heard myself saying, "He's honest and I think he is willing to reveal himself."

"Who is?" Jean said.

"Gerhardt."

"I thought you meant André."

"Well I may also mean André."

I didn't say of course compared to Oskar, Gerhardt was practically lying on an analytic couch.

"Sounds like you were more intimate over dinner than two years with you know—" Jean said.

I smiled.

"But if he's had so much pain in his past, he's going to drive toward it in a relationship. He's going to bring about his own pain again," Marguerite said. "That's what he knows."

André said, "Oh come on Marguerite. All relationships end up with pain anyway."

"They do?" I asked.

"Or he could be empathic and self-aware," Jean answered.

"He's a man," Marguerite contradicted her, with annoyance.

One shouldn't discuss relationships with novelists, I realized. They go right to the last chapter quickly.

I myself had also wondered if he was just good at the beginning of a relationship. But who isn't?

"But, we return in a few days, you know that?" Marguerite said, lifting her head. The waiters in their white jackets were scurrying around us, taking away side plates and empty glass jars of jam.

"Yes. I know. It's sad. I meet a man who suits me and I have to leave."

"I feel exactly the same way," Marguerite said.

My head jerked up. Then I said, "You two don't have to leave."

Jean asked, "Why ARE we going back?"

Marguerite said, "She has to build a career."

Jean shrugged. "Oh that . . ." as if it was silly. At least they meant back to the U.S. when they were discussing leaving.

"Yes," Jean said teasingly, "We must take steps to keep you two together." She turned to Marguerite, "What are we going to do about it?"

"Anyway," I said. "The real problem is I can't afford to pop over to Vienna all the time."

"Well, till you see him again," Jean said, "write. That is the way to warm oneself in the night. While one is waiting for life to play a hand. You know," she said, "if you sit back, be quiet and let life happen, it can deal new hands that are quite surprising. Happy hands, darling."

Marguerite looked a bit suspiciously at her. "Anyway, it's all well and good," Marguerite said, "that your love life is at least a bit more romantic but your work life has to also improve. We have to write a book together. One that sells."

"You sound like Oskar," I said.

"Exactly," Marguerite replied, gloating. Proof she was backing the right horse.

Marguerite looked at her watch. "I love working in hotels," she said. "Let's go spend three hours in our rooms writing." She looked at André.

"Or whatever you're going to be doing," Jean said. She looked at me. "Good. I already started something."

"Me too," Marguerite said, pushing her chair out and gathering up her glasses and the book she was carrying. I peered over. Dave Eggers.

"Like it?" I asked.

"Very good to start, then it drones on a bit. Americans all write incessantly about their terrible childhoods as if they are surprised life is painful. Of course it's painful. This obsession with youth is about refusing the real life of adulthood. Childhood is in the imagination. Americans don't want to write about the responsibilities of an adult heart."

Then she looked at me questioningly.

"Don't worry," I said. "I'm writing, too."

"Due to our situation," Jean said, "it is not so important what we are writing since one can't publish posthumously—well, one can but it would be such a legal case. Where did these documents come from, people would think it was forgery, acts of imagination, which they are—"

"You could publish under another name," André said.

"I like my own name," Jean said. "Anyway once you're in our situation all this self-gratification of publishing, notoriety is not so important. I like the writing itself. Don't you Marguerite?"

She was thinking, standing up ready to go. André was standing up too. She said, "But it would be lucrative you know to have these people think they found posthumous works because they would sell incredibly well, you understand that?" she said to Jean. "We'd make quite a bit of money."

"But who would be collecting the money?" Jean asked.

I regret to say I had myself wondered who does receive their royalties. I am still, after all, living on the earthly plane with far too many earthly bills.

"You," Marguerite pointed to me, "must make something, or you will die."

"But you did and you died."

"I meant you'll die inside," she said. "Anyway it is because of the work we did that we came back to life. Keep that in mind."

Jean looked at Marguerite and André. André seemed quite comfortable about going with Marguerite to her bedroom. As noted, he is French. I suppose that is where all conversations end.

Jean said, "I'll work in the lobby."

"You mean the bar," Marguerite said smiling.

Marguerite in bed. Jean in the bar. Their "work" seemed to be shifting rather quickly to their favorite preoccupations.

In my own room, I drank 4 coffees. What would I write about? That's what I didn't know. I picked up one of Marguerite's books because she was always writing about writing. "*Nowadays it often seems writing is nothing at all. Sometimes I realize that if writing isn't, all things, all contraries confounded, a quest for vanity and void, it's nothing. That if it's not each time, all things confounded into one through some inexpressible essence, then writing is nothing but advertisement. But usually I have no opinion, I can see that all options are open now, that there seem to be no more barriers, that writing seems at a loss for somewhere to hide, to be written, to be read. That its basic unseemliness is no longer accepted. But at that point I stop thinking about it.*" Yes, I could see that.

I called my machine in New York to check for messages. Telemarketing calls. Wonderful. I am paying long distance rates to pick up impersonal voice activated recordings. Why did I really think I had to be in New York anyway? What the hell was so important there?

I began to write about being sad and how wonderful a tall man is. How wonderful a tall man is. No good.

I looked out the window, it was snowing. The first snowfall.

What they both lived through, because the truth is, it is what I lived through, also.

When Jean moved as a young girl from the Caribbean, penniless, odd, too intense, frightened, she became a chorus girl to make money. I didn't do that, when I left Montreal for the States, I was too shy, but, like her, I was also broke and lived off men's stares. That's why they hired me to be their secretaries, their assistants. I certainly never had any qualifications, although I had the diligence of someone who needs to earn her daily bread.

These men bought me dinner, proposed jewelry, affairs, marriage. When nothing was forthcoming from me, they left me alone, not bothering one whit what happened to me. As indeed I thought I deserved.

Jean and I hadn't been strong enough to hold a man's interest when we were young. We were not formed enough. There was not enough of a whole person to love. Jean had lodged inside her the pain of being an outcast in her country and a mother's lack of love and made a cocktail from that by holding onto a cocktail. She did, however, have a future of solitary writing in front of her. So she danced, I waited tables and typed, and we relied on these men's kindnesses. We knew they were not long lasting. We were trying to take care of ourselves. In Paris, she met Ford Madox Ford, who told her to write. She did and she knocked him out. She was a natural and he was not.

And Marguerite? She did have men who loved her when she was young. Marguerite was stronger than Jean and I. Maybe this André loved her. Maybe he still does. I certainly hope they were making love now. Her romantic demise came after her fifties. There was just she, drink and the sea. How odd that Marguerite's lover had the same last name as Jean's first husband, Jean Lenglet. Eventually Marguerite's love, François Lenglet, died from ill health. After writing a successful novel himself. Then she was with the gay man, Yann Steiner, who lived with her till her death. He loved her. She loved him. But he did not love her as a woman. Why did Marguerite like Oskar? That French attitude of admiring someone who is out for himself? I wasn't the type. I was the type who prides herself on taking nothing, the pride of the disinherited.

This wasn't the case with Marguerite, who knew she was rich, rich with talent. She could be arrogant.

I couldn't afford to be arrogant. I don't know why not. It just wasn't my way.

Gerhardt appeared to have a heart. It could be a new reckoning.

Hadn't we all come here for a new reckoning? Wasn't a new reckoning how you moved new squares on the checkerboard?

I must force myself to go with that, I told myself.

FIFTEEN

We were walking through the Vienna shopping area again. The sun was out but it was cold and we were all sick of fastening our coats in tightly around us, bucking ourselves up against the ice chill. Just months now till Spring. I hoped Jean and Marguerite would still be here, on the planet. They had to re-experience Spring. That aliveness. That liberation. It would be wonderful to see them making their way among pale lilacs and pink and white fulsome peonies, walking slowly in the gentle sun-filled air.

We three turned as one unit into the bookshop. And there was some hoopla, in the English section, about mother's day. It wasn't mother's day, that's in May. Did the Austrians have a different day?

Both Jean and Marguerite stood and looked at the sappy cards for sale. They were quiet, as if looking at graves. They'd each had one child. Jean was a lousy mother, and sent her daughter off to the ex-con father, who raised her quite well. Maryvonne was her daughter's name and she took care of her mother late in life, as daughters often do for mothers who were useless to them. Let me show you how it is done.

Marguerite had a son, Outi, by Dionys, her husband's friend, who may have been the love of her life, although he cheated on her constantly. But then she was cheating on her husband with him. This was Paris, enough said. Marguerite always had an uneasy relationship with her men. Most of them could not settle into her passion, her demands, her intensity. She let nothing lie. But as far as her son was concerned, she took such delight in every aspect of motherhood, cooking the meals, watching him learn to walk, speak, grow. She loved her son as passionately as she loved her men, and ended up making films, making art, with him. What an artist will do with someone they love.

I did not have a child, as you know. I did not have the courage. But was that disavowal and refusal why I had not succeeded, as they had, as a writer? They went the distance in love, even if botching up here and there. And with their work too, without the botching. (I was forgetting at that moment the countless geniuses, who had no children. Or maybe I was not forgetting that I am not a genius.)

"Well I am close to my ex's daughter," I said, defensively.

"You never mention your husband," Jean said.

"Well we were together twenty years, five of them married. I loved him, he is a marvelous person, but he wanted a child and I thought I wanted to be alone. We both got what we allegedly wanted. In his case, happily. In my case, not."

"A common story for neurotics," Marguerite replied.

"Yes," I said.

I too began fingering the silly cards. I am not my ex's daughter's mother. I am sort of her aunt, the little girl would explain if asked. I have spoiled her, Lila, unmercifully, bought her doll's clothes and meals and plays and taxi rides, as if she is a queen, because she is lively and smart and Oskar, who has met her, thinks she is an elf. It is her magical quality, as if everything is splendiferous.

Maybe it is.

I smiled in the bookshop. I remembered the sight of Lila showing Oskar, by his fireplace, each one of her doll outfits, very meticulously, the shoes, the bag, the leg warmers, this for ballet, this for fiesta and he listening attentively and asking her about the presidents of the periods from which her dolls hailed from. She had a Civil War doll. A Fifties doll. You name it. Then he advised her to only accept valentines from the republicans in her third grade class.

She was laughing at his gibberish and talking to him, showing me how his kaleidoscope, which sat on his windowsill, worked, even though it is I, who have been there many times and this was her first visit. She made her way round his apartment as if she was a frequent guest.

It almost made me cry standing here now in Vienna thinking about them together. She played the piano for him plus sang him a song in her little voice. I don't remember the song because when children sing songs they all sound as if they're singing the same song.

Lila wears her hats as my ex wore his, with aplomb. As Oskar wears his. Maybe they are all a different race.

But then my ex decided he didn't like me being so close to his nine-year-old daughter. He stopped the relationship. She and I always used to have "dates", where like an attentive much older lover, I showered gifts and attention. My ex and his wife began putting the kibosh on the dates. He did not want me influencing her, showing her lives that he himself was not living. She was to be his imprint alone. I had said No child, and I must bear my fate.

They started saying Lila was busy, when I asked about a date. And now when I lie down and want to think of pure love, when I used to conjure up her face, I feel I am not allowed to anymore. Even Lila is a bit distant now with me when I am given a pass to take her for lobster or for a smoothie, having heard her parents discuss me in god knows what terms.

I looked over at my friends in the bookshop. They too were uniquely silent and somber. I wanted to say, Maybe Maryvonne and Outi can come back too. Why wouldn't they if you can? Maybe they are happy wherever they are. Don't be sad.

I remembered lines from one of Marguerite's books, it might be *Emily L.* "*We weren't looking at anything. You ordered some tea. I said, 'Sometimes I think that's all there is. Sometimes I think it's all over. More all over than anyone can imagine. The only sign of life is the thought of death.'*

"*'Yes. Death. We can't bear it. But for you it's nothing. Put yourself in my place.'*

"We can laugh again at death. We look at the bridge at Tancarville, the pink above the sea."

Now the author was dead and she, with Jean Rhys, were staring blindly at Mother's day cards. But the pain in these women's hearts was that they could never be with their children anymore. Those little faces, the funny things they say, their willingness to cleave to you, their wild enjoyment in everything they do, from cutting up old clothing to ordering spring rolls.

I looked at Jean who was running her hand over her face, as if to tell herself she really was here. I don't think Jean's mother was accessible, distant from everyone since she was stuck on a Caribbean island and poor and hated by the natives, and so Jean's mother decided to not like her daughter, there had to be some response to how she herself was not liked. Marguerite's mother was fierce, but cold to her daughter. Like most of the French, her mind was consumed with money. And men. Men, in Marguerite's mother's case, meant her sons. Not her daughter.

I looked out the window at the plaza below. Trying to distract myself. Take away the feeling. I should send Lila a gift, a card, something.

I thought of Gerhardt. How I had tried to tell him there is an ensuing violence to the self in the decision to not have a child.

Oskar had had a child so he knew how to be with children. Why he was so good with Lila. When I had been in love with Oskar, I wished I could have had his child but I was too old. At this point in our lives, we had to be content with child's play.

When I first spent time with Oskar, he had sat across a table from me and began talking about Kokoschka's doll of Alma Mahler. How Kokoschka carried it around with him to the opera, to parties. I told him that Kokoschka threw the doll out a window. Oskar did not know that. Now that I think about it, who else talks about a life size doll with such relish? It amazed Oskar that I knew about it. And I was amazed at what I thought was his positivity, his humor, his love of life. It lifts the heart. There is absolutely no reason why every woman wouldn't be in love with him, I thought. He's handsome, rich, witty, adventurous, with a sense for art.

I could hear him; "I renew myself, Mira, with reading. That is why I don't want to be together all the time."

Of course, he was lying.

At the time I thought he was saying he himself wanted a life size doll, not a real woman and her untimely feelings.

"Why do you keep thinking about the same old things?" Marguerite asked sidling up to me, as if listening to my inner voice. I swallowed guiltily.

She continued, "You play the same old tapes. You will be abandoned, you are not good enough for him, you cannot be the first string in his life . . . Why do you do this to yourself?"

I shrugged. Were they forgetting we had just seen him with another woman?

"But who knows what that woman means to Oskar?" Marguerite said. "Maybe he did come to see you. You jumped to the worst case and then to the worst . . ." she looked at my face, "doctor."

I cringed and touched my face. It wasn't hot anymore and the swelling had gone down and now I just looked old, like I used to before I spent all that money.

"It is possible a man can love you," she said. "But you have to start having more emotions."

"Like what?"

"Desire . . . you have to let yourself feel it."

I blushed. How do they know everything? I am often aloof with Oskar.

Suddenly in my mind's eye, I saw us in his bed. Me on top of him, his hands fast by his side, my body all alone up there, moving up and down, never a kiss, never his hands all over me, his eyes shut tight as if he didn't want to see me. He'd move away when, after, I fell over him, and dared to kiss him on the cheek. Did I not want to see me, also? Did I not want to exist?

He never touched me. And I allowed it.

We were in collusion. I should have asked him, I should have asked him to touch me. To break into myself. Isn't that what a man's supposed to do? Enter you in every way?

I turned to Marguerite and Jean. Jean was reading incredulously the Mother's day cards, shocked at their insipidness. Marguerite had moved off into philosophy.

Finally, Marguerite called out to Jean, "Outi used to ask me as a child, what is heaven like?"

Jean looked over. "What did you answer?"

"I quoted Miriam Makeba. That song. '*You can't go there by a bike or a car it's across the moon, beyond the stars . . .*'"

Neither Jean nor I said anything.

"And as the song goes," Marguerite said, "'*I could have said if I know your daddy, he's saved a place for you.*' Not that Dionys was dead then. But we're all dead, aren't we, sooner."

Jean nodded.

All of a sudden I started crying like a child and I was not the one who had lost a child. I was the one who hadn't been one or was still one. I became overwhelmed with tears. One needs love when one is alive, there's no getting away from it, and one has to try, and evidently one needs love even after one is dead.

I had cried in the elevator on the way to that doctor at losing Oskar and then I had cried this morning walking to meet Jean and Marguerite at losing Oskar and now I was crying at the possibility of losing Lila, just by her growing up and her possessive father. They both glanced at me.

As if to say, don't think we don't know.

SIXTEEN

Jean, unbelievably, had figured out the internet on my Blackberry. She was checking how many of her books were selling on Amazon. Marguerite had her do the same for her books. They both were thrilled. They are more popular now than then and it was exhilarating.

We were in the bar of the Hotel Sacher and Jean said, "It makes one feel so alive to have one's work received. Doesn't it?"

Marguerite also quickly became adept on my Blackberry and was not to be spoken with. She was reading a plethora of customer reviews that, unlike most current reviews, were not written by her friends.

That's when André walked in, sat down and quietly, like me, simply watched them fiddling with, as people like to call them, my device.

I said, "There are probably websites devoted to both of you, too."

"What?" Jean asked. "Really? Under our names?"

I took the Blackberry from Marguerite and typed in each one of their names and there were about thirty Google entries for each writer.

"I will lend you my computer upstairs, and go online for you—"

"You mean anyone can connect to this central repository of information?" Marguerite asked, excited.

"Yes. We'll do each one of you one night and you can stay up reading all about yourselves. We'll see how accurate it all is."

"How extraordinary," Jean said.

"It's rather invasive," Marguerite added, but I could tell she liked seeing all the entries about her.

"So everyone is a celebrity on this box?" Jean asked, rather presciently I thought.

"In their own mind," I responded.

"Not really," Marguerite said. "People are reading it so it's in other minds, too."

"In both your cases, yes, but in other people's no. They're busy hoping everyone is reading about them but I don't know if people are. Maybe they are. Maybe people inevitably find each other who are of the same sensibility and that is the whole social networking zeitgeist."

"Mass exhibitionism," Marguerite said, laughing.

"Exactly . . . Well, it's not only that. There is a repository of information which everyone can access in seconds which can be useful but it's a funny thing . . . when you can get information so easily, you are not sure whether to trust it."

Jean said, "It's like when a man falls in love too easily. One doesn't trust it either."

"Precisely," I said, thinking Gerhardt seemed to be falling for me rather quickly. Why? What could he have possibly seen?

"What's wrong with falling in love too easily?" Marguerite asked. "André, you have fallen in love easily in your life, haven't you?"

"Of course," he said smiling, sipping his coffee.

"How long did it last?" I asked.

"In one case," he said, "twenty years."

"You see?" Marguerite said. "You two are too suspicious. Of everything." Then she looked at my Blackberry. "I for one look forward to reading what the box says."

Jean said, "Nobody knew about me much when I was alive."

"There's even a play about you," I said to Jean. I turned to Marguerite, "Quite a few films about you. You and Yann Steiner. They made a stupid film of *The Lover*. Although everyone loved the look of the actress. Of you young, so to speak."

"I don't want to see those," she said. "They will be all wrong."

They sipped their coffees staring at my Blackberry like it was an alive thing. Which it is because it kept beeping every time an email came in. Our eyes kept returning to it and I hate to say it but every time it rang I was hoping it was Oskar. Habit, I suppose. That was how we communicated.

"Look at it," Marguerite ordered me, as if there might be an email for her.

Jean said dreamily, "It is wonderful though to have such attention." And I nodded. I had to admit Gerhardt's continual interest in me, as he called or sent me messages or insisted on seeing me, was rebuilding, inch by inch, my feeling of being valuable.

And Marguerite was far more cheerful now that André was about, even if only silently, respectfully basking in all this female energy.

I opened my emails. "Oh look at this," I said. It was from a woman I had hired to get my play going. She was writing that perhaps she had found an angel investor and we could possibly go up this summer. I quickly emailed, "Who?" pushed Send, and delightedly sat back and smiled at them. "They may have money for my play. Can you imagine?"

I was also all of a sudden feeling energetic and hopeful about life in art. Not to mention, I could not get over that here we were sitting in a blue bar in a Viennese hotel and they were softly playing Isaac Hayes on the speaker. A black ghetto guy in Mozart's hotel? Proving that art, no matter what you think it is, will come alive somewhere. You might be dead, it might be another country . . . But something will happen.

"So what are you and André doing tonight?" I asked Marguerite.

"We are introducing Jean to an Englishman. We met him in the bar. He's perfect for Jean."

"English?" I repeated, smiling.

Marguerite rubbed her skirt, "She likes Englishmen. His name is Robin. Very solid, rich, old like us but Cambridge educated. Admires writers so he will love her. He could take care of her while we're here."

"She doesn't need taking care of," I said.

Jean said, "We all need taking care of."

It was futile to debate that. We finished our teas and then decided to go to our rooms to write. They had dates tonight, it seemed.

So they were busy writing. I was too and this possibility of some hope for my play stimulated me.

We now felt we weren't writing in the dark. There was someone out there listening. But as I sat there at my desk in my room with the heavy brocaded curtains blocking out the light, I still wasn't sure what to write about. My outer life was too full. The three of us had gone to a concert the night before in St. Stephen's Square in a church, Beethoven's *Missa Solemnis*, and it turned out that many of the people attending the concert were in black tie. One man was very handsome and Jean said he was rich as Croesus; she seemed to know who he was. A very rich Hebraic man, she said. Well, he was tall, had wonderful hair and an aristocratic face (although he had made his money in whiskey, Jean said approvingly). He stood casually over his chair at the intermission, confident and good. She said he was an incredible philanthropist.

And then I imagined a story where I met him, and of course now that I look like a monster at least in my own mind, he wouldn't be attracted to me, and we have to admit his wife was very attractive with very long dark hair, slender, but in my imagination his father turned out to have had an affair with my Viennese mother. Perhaps I was his half sister, and he writes me a check for my play to go up which was no money to him at all and then threw in, on a whim, an extra $750K for me. In my story, I start to cry while talking to him. Why do I do that? Oh yes, because he tells me I am a beautiful older woman, that was why he gave me the money, not because of my mother although I added that thought in a bit later, but because I am beautiful as an older woman which he thought was far more worthy of affirmation, it was easy to be beautiful when young. Oskar and Mr. Philanthropist's wife would be watching us from another room wondering what was going on. Oskar. Always popping up. In real life or in my stories.

Again *Emily L.* came to mind: "*I haven't decided anything . . . but that's not the point. I can't stop writing. I can't. And when I'm writing the story it's as if I were back with you again, back at a time when I don't know yet what's happening or what's going to happen . . . who you are or what is going to become of us.*"

I deliberated what next in my story, although all this sounded a bit Danielle Steele, whose books certainly had not been bad luck for her.

Well, at least the pondering was pleasant. I no longer wanted to write about how terrible my mother or father had been. Those years were long gone.

A knock on my hotel room door. Maybe room service although I had not ordered up tea or coffee. It was only 3 in the afternoon. I walked across the soft carpet. I had put my hair up which made my face slightly less awful. I don't know why.

Gerhardt was standing there with pink and white flowers. He almost looked like the man in my fantasy from the concert last night.

"Come in," I said, delighted.

"I am sorry to disturb you," he said. "I just left the rehearsal and have a few hours before we play tonight."

He had a soft sweater on. Tapered slacks. His longish grey hair a bit shaggy, as if he didn't have time to think about it.

"I don't feel disturbed at all. Thrilled," I said. I had always been so careful with Oskar. Not to frighten him. But my timidity had only exacerbated the distance between us. Not now, I wouldn't. As the poet Ko Un wrote: "*Ask and ask until nothing's left to ask.*"

Gerhardt looked down at me. I had taken off my sweater and was wearing a very low cut pink t-shirt. One I used to wear with such grace and beauty when young. Now it was one I had to usually cover up if I went out. One's breasts get bigger and more pendulous as one gets older.

"Would you like to go out after the concert tonight?" he asked, still standing in my room. "Dinner? At 10.30?"

"Of course, of course," I said. And then I stood up from sitting on the bed listening to him, so he would be less lonely up there all alone. I suddenly became flustered. "How was the rehearsal?"

He stood a bit taller; now, we were in his world and it was all more manageable. "Excellent. We are playing *Carmina Burana* tonight with a Spanish chorus."

"Do you like that piece?" I asked.

"It's amusing. It's a crowd pleaser, even in Vienna."

"Wait," I said, "I thought Orff was a Nazi."

He stiffened. "Not a Nazi but he was not against the regime."

I had suddenly got myself into difficult territory. I wasn't in the mood for a philo-Semitic discussion, as Jean would say. I couldn't believe that a great composer wanted to kill Jews.

Gerhardt looked cannily at me. "He was in Germany and he wanted to stay on in his country. Perhaps he closed his eyes but that is what people did to not be hauled off or lose their homes. It is difficult to understand in after thought."

I began frantically thinking of Bonhoeffer, the Christian pastor, the one Christian pastor, who fought against the regime, smuggling out information to England, to terrible ends for himself. I didn't want to do this. Let me think about music, I told myself, quite aware I was doing precisely what Carl Orff might have been doing.

I focused instead on Gerhardt's perfect oval face. His sensitive eyes. His well-shaped mouth. His clear blue eyes. His long legs.

"Great," he said. "I'll see you tonight. I will meet you here."

And I leaned up and kissed his cheek. "You're what's great," I said. "You've made me happy."

He smiled, like a boy, and said nothing. And that was when I knew he had been practicing the oboe all his life, not spending his time chasing women. He was embarrassed and the courting of a woman was not an unknown thing to him, but it was not something tired and predictable, either. Probably it had been women who had courted him. And he had gone along with it, not having time or faith perhaps to choose his own love. The women had come to him and then he had to find out if he wanted them. And sometimes he hadn't. And then he had, as we all do, problems. But here he was, choosing me.

All three of us would be out on dates tonight.

And, like Sara in the Bible being told she would have a baby at 90 years old, I laughed.

That evening, late, we went to a small restaurant and he had a hamburger, how odd, and I had mussels and we had a drink and we spoke about music. I told him about my play about Mahler and he was interested although not that fond of Mahler, it turned out. Not because he was Jewish I hoped. No, no, he said, he found much of the music sentimental.

It was not necessary he like Mahler. I didn't know if I liked Mahler so much myself (but I did, I did—I was addicted to the ninth) but I was fond of my play and the theatricality to come of getting it up.

"Are you looking forward to the play being shown?" he asked.

"If it really does get shown."

"What do you mean?" he asked attentively. (Oskar only had faint interest in anything I did. He would zone out or move onto discussing other subjects immediately if any of my own projects were discussed at the table.) Now I wondered if that was some kind of sensitivity, some kind of trying to be open-minded towards my magical machinations.

"Well I have learned through all this that the characters around getting the play up in a theatre are more involved and tricky than the characters on the pages of the play," I said.

"You should write a play about that," he laughed.

"Noel Coward did a helluva lot better than I ever could. And also with a play you have to listen to so many people's opinions. It seems that whomever is funding the money trumps those who are not."

I looked over at Gerhardt finishing his American hamburger, and I was a little confounded how someone who played a string instrument, as Gerhardt did, could not love Mahler's music.

"I'm surprised you don't like Mahler," I said. "I thought he wrote so the musicians could really play out." I was still nervous, I could tell, that it was because Gustav was Jewish. I remember hearing that the Weiner Philharmoniker would not play Mahler for Bernstein (two Jews in one Austrian concert hall) till Bernstein stopped, stood at the podium, and stared at them challengingly. They began to play.

"There are movements that I like less than others," I continued about Mahler, "but that is true for all artists. But there are some beautiful parts," I asserted, remembering my favorite parts are allegedly the ones where Mahler foresaw his own death.

Have they come to get me? I suddenly wondered again. Why was this thought reappearing? Of course that is why they are here. Dead people always show themselves to people who are dying themselves. Sitting here it now became clear that what was going on, Jean and Marguerite had come to get me. This was a last chance at life and then, poof. I suddenly felt terrified and clutched my drink (much like my mentors). Then what I felt surprised me. It wasn't a man I began thinking about. That I must have a perfect relationship before I bump off. No, what I was thinking was that I must write something good before they take me. God, I hope they give me the chance to get that done.

I quickly turned to Gerhardt who was saying, "Yes you like some of Mahler but that says something about Mahler. There is no Beethoven that I do not like. Maybe Fidelio. Maybe not," he mused. "No Bach I do not like."

I was enjoying this musing. It stopped me from my own. I am being ridiculous, I told myself. I am not ready to go.

"There is no Vaughan Williams I do not like," I said.

He smiled, amused that I wanted to play with him. I am not sure he was used to playing with people offstage.

Should I sleep with him? I wondered. I should not hold onto Oskar like that. Still I had enjoyed being faithful to Oskar.

I had enjoyed loving one man, even if it didn't seem that he loved me. I now understood the aristocracy of loving one man, giving all of yourself to another. There is no other way, I realized. The rest is juggling and subterfuge.

We finished dinner and Gerhardt said, "What would you like to do now?"

"Maybe I should get back to the hotel," I found myself saying, in spite of myself. So the truth was, I saw, I was frightened to begin a new story.

He smiled graciously. It made me think maybe he doesn't expect to go to bed just because one has dinner together. He deserved more passion from me but maybe even he would agree it is better to be conscientious, aware of, and serious about the shoals when embarking on romance. I hadn't gone slowly with Oskar. I had been so willing—although guardedly—to jump off the cliff. And it is, let's face it, a marvelous experience to lose one's self like that.

I turned toward Gerhardt and thought, This is not the end. Although I had no idea what I was actually referring to. It could have been a multiplicity of things. My life. My love for Oskar. My potential with Gerhardt. The story I was writing. Who knew?

When we got up to go, I took his arm and held it warmly, safe in his splendor.

And I smiled up at him, and meant it, and it was sweet to look at him, and whatever we were doing, I thought, we are trying to be ourselves. We took a leisurely walk home together and often we were silent and I didn't mind it, it felt more intimate than if we had been talking. We passed a bookstore and looked in the windows and I followed the German titles of novels I knew, playing a game to myself of what they were in English, as children name cars they pass from the back seat. We passed shops and I looked at the clothes and they were not really my style, this wasn't Florence or Paris, but it was fun to just walk and then we got to the hotel and he kissed me lightly good night and it was another lovely evening.

There is time, I told myself, going up alone in the elevator.

And I was aware that I was contradicting exactly what I had got myself in a stew about at dinner. Now I was telling myself there is time to wait for what is good.

And the day had brought some of that. The possible funding. And my not running away from Gerhardt and the sweetness of feeling love for my two friends.

Both of whose lights were out when I passed their doors.

They were still not home, it seemed.

I suspected that even though they might have had their brushes with sobriety when they were alive, I think they were eschewing it this go round. And why not? Why not enjoy life now in the way you want to, in all one's particular eccentricities and particular proclivities? That was also curiously obvious at this moment and something, like death, that seemed to be so easy to forget.

SEVENTEEN

Duras when drunk had made ugly phone calls to writers she was jealous of, denigrating their reviews, challenging their integrity. She made phone calls to past lovers who had betrayed her, why, why had they done this to her. She had screamed, clawed, cried, and said unforgettable truths to Dionys when she found out he was cheating. After they broke up, she got involved with a journalist, Lenglet, with whom she wrote films. He was married to someone else but he and Marguerite were dedicated to one another. Yet they regularly slapped each other's faces, pulled each other's hair, shoved and tried to hurt the other physically and of course mentally. In bars. In the car. In hotel bedrooms.

Jean's first husband was good to her; he bought her gifts, tried to tend to her, admired her, but lied incessantly. She had been young, and he had been gentle with her. She wasn't used to these doting attentions (he was Belgian) after having just lost herself to the cold calculations, the lack of romanticism of an Englishman. But she never really knew what her husband did for a living. There is much violence in lying to someone who loves you. He ended up in prison and her third husband, a Colonel in the British army, also ended up in prison for bank fraud. She had loved this husband, too. He was kind and cared for her. Just deeply flawed.

In her drinking, I think with her second husband, who was not violent but worn and embattled from tending to her, she herself ended up in prison, a prison hospital. She had flown at him violently in an argument. That frenzy of the disenfranchised. She lashed out in her agony.

I lashed out to my face.

I once punched my ex-husband, a good patient man who somehow had landed himself with a difficult woman (me). I had punched him when I was too angry to speak. I cannot even remember why I was so angry, no doubt I felt he was not loving me as he should, and I could not bear the pain so I asked him to roll down his car window and I smacked him. Oskar told me a girlfriend who was a model pulled a knife on him. He had to call the police. That was after she had punched in some walls and I think he mentioned another woman broke all his lamps. Another time some woman whom he was seducing went a little nuts on him and would not leave his bathtub. He was frightened, he said, she would jump from the balcony. Here he was running a NASDAQ company, he said, and it would be in the headlines.

This is what happens between men and women. When they are in love. Or maybe better stated when we are in need. The hurt between us, or the hurt that loving makes us remember, can turn us violent.

How many men had I just walked out on? It's a violence, too.

I looked up at Gerhardt the next night at dinner, when we once again went out after his concert.

"What are you reading?" he asked.

"A manuscript by a friend about a murder in a night club. Lots of abuse in the story. Some survived it and some don't." Will I get violent with him when he hurts me, I wondered. "What are you reading?" I continued.

"I started reading Heinrich Böll again."

"Oh I love him," I said. "The one with the different viewpoints about the woman, I forget the title."

Will he cheat on me when he is angry that I am old and no longer beautiful? Will that be his violence?

"You mean *Group Portrait with Lady*," he said.

"Yes." What ugliness is in store for us as he speaks so kindly and softly and willingly to me now? "Yes, thank you."

He smiled and took my hand and we were silent. I thought this time, this time I will behave. He was no doubt thinking the same about himself. But of course, I knew we wouldn't. I sipped my wine and thought, at least let me behave with some modicum of patience and stability right now. I can only do that, take the gentlest and most loving action in the moment. I will be my best self, hourly, till the angry child stomps her foot and wants to break everything between us just for the way he didn't phrase a sentence thoughtfully enough. Let me behave estimably while I can. Let me behave estimably, I said to myself, as his eyes kept returning to the framed drawings of buttocks above me in the restaurant.

EIGHTEEN

When Jean was poor in Paris and her husband in prison for forgery, she would visit him. Go to the prison on the bus and wait in the waiting room, be body checked for contraband, and sit with him on wooden chairs and study his nervous face. He promised that he would take care of her when he got out, that their lives would change, she would never have to live so vulnerably again, he promised her everything, as people who have nothing often do.

She ended up living with Ford Madox Ford. The great man, who was a successful editor and overseer of some literary talent in Paris, recognized her talent and encouraged her, sometimes changing her sentences. He also slept with her. The big Englishman, the Englishman whom she loved, like my mother did, she too loved Englishmen, my mother and Jean, both felt secure with that perfect use of language, not to mention the mellifluous accents. Or maybe it was that the Englishmen won wars. Or, even more likely, those boarding schools made these men riven for women.

Ford's wife knew what was going on, but looked away. Maybe Ford was difficult. Every man a woman loves is difficult. Each man is strangled in the way he loves, frightened of strangling and being strangled himself.

Eventually Ford grew tired of Jean's neediness, her timidity, her dependence on him. He began to distance from her. But he published the book Jean wrote about them; *Quartet*, and Jean went back to her husband when he got out of prison. Her husband left her again, this time to work in Holland and to raise their daughter. He knew and told Jean that he had nothing to offer her, and asked her to return to England. She should go write.

I was thinking about all of this at Mahler's *Symphony No. 9* last night, which I was attending at the Musikverein with a friend, who just happens to be in Vienna.

"What are you writing?" Alexandra asked, between the performance of Mahler's *9th* and the *10th*.

It wasn't the Weiner Philharmoniker playing that night. It was the London Philharmonic, which does not have a conductor. Just guest conductors. You can't tell those Brits anything.

Gerhardt does not like Mahler so he was not with us. He had said to me, "In years past I would have gone with you to hear him, feeling this was a way to get close to you, but now I don't feel it is necessary."

"It isn't," I said. And I meant it. If we did get close, it would be without having to sacrifice any truths of whom we are.

"I'm writing about Duras and Rhys," I answered Alexandra to see what she would say. Alexandra is in her late seventies, a white Russian and she had been a textile designer. She has tremendous aesthetics. She never had a CD or record player. She went to live concerts all her life. She has seen them all. Von Karajan. Bernstein. Claudio Abbado. When she speaks of music, her shoulders lift, her hands fly to her heart, it as if each performance was a private love affair.

She said, "I never liked Rhys. She was too much the victim. Living off men. Too yearning for them as saviors."

I nodded. I decided not to say anything about how close I am to these women. Alexandra would think I am mad. The lights began dimming and I squirmed nervously. I could feel that, in the internalization of the music, I, too, might begin to wonder if I am mad. The music would do that; give me the infinite time to explore.

Finally, I said, "I don't see Jean like that." I looked around at that moment at the people in the concert hall getting ready for the next program, as if all we attendees were one giant bird settling our feathers in, to begin listening again. "What is the point of one's independence anyway?" I continued. "Yes, yes, you get to live alone and you teach yourself to do things alone but the sweetness, there is another sweetness, in the longing for and being with a man. In the feeling vulnerable, just by one's own willingness, one's own yearning. Love undoes. And it is good to be undone."

"What on earth do you mean?" Alexandra said, shocked. She swung her blunt cut hair towards me, as she asked.

"Feeling strong in oneself is good, I admit," I answered, "but redundant. That kind of strength is constant, yes, but it's defended, has no motion. The feeling of desire, the longing, is liquid and probably does lead to no good but it is what happens between a man and a woman, and Jean let it happen."

I felt I was losing Alexandra as a friend as I said this. But I knew she had longed for men in her own past, had had lovers, husbands, been hurt. So why was she against a woman admitting to those feelings? But I did not ask. Sometimes it is not necessary to prod into someone's private memories and thoughts. Let them tell you if they want to. Their reveries belong to them. I am not her therapist.

Anyway, whom is anyone kidding? Jean was no passive victim. Not with sentences like tigers. Her strength was in her art. She was powerful there and exhausted in life.

Just as Mahler was, as he wrote this music. His wife was cheating. His heart was failing in more ways than one and yet he wrote this sublimity. All the artists were paying the bills, fighting with spouses, while trying to create transcendence. I would hardly call that passive.

I turned to Alexandra and said, "Jean's characters in her book, all her books, were leaving or being left by the Mr. Mackenzies. Her women characters perhaps didn't want to be left or alone, but they all ended up leaving the Mr. Mackenzies, only to end up being themselves. Because they were all fundamentally honest and could not prevaricate."

Alexandra shot me a glance as if to say, What is going on with you?

The music instantly began and we both were taken. I closed my eyes and I began wondering again, how is it I am spending my time with two dead writers? Is this imagination or is this wondrousness? And, come to think of it, as the music began to move insistently, what is the difference?

I opened my eyes, looked at the orchestra blindly, only hearing the music, and closed my eyes again. It doesn't matter if it's true or not, just like with God. What matters is the feeling and what you learn when you believe. The infinite options and gifts and possibilities that you cannot reckon but unexpectedly come alive when you believe.

NINETEEN

Marguerite and I were in the lobby. Maybe it was one or two in the morning. I was tired since I had also not been able to sleep the night before. I had been worrying. How am I going to support myself? How am I going to survive? Oskar had always referred to me as an outlier and it was true. I had not planned on a future when young, perhaps so depressed as a child, I could not think ahead. It had taken everything I had to get through the moments I was living through. It had taken all of me. I had banked on the purity and freedom of art as a mitigating factor against all the unhappiness I had seen. I was internal, driven, driven to words and insights. I just had not known that that low self-esteem in me was not bankable. How had these two women done it? That was the real question.

Was that vision I had had inside when I was young of myself as an artist real? Or delusion? I had done the work, so that was not delusion but the actualizing of it, had that been my imagination or had I indeed seen into my future something silent and true waiting for me as an eventuality?

"You know what I love about your work?" I asked Marguerite to distract myself and maybe her from my problems. We were still sitting in the opulent and rich lobby, both lost in thought. By now it must be past 2 in the morning, I thought. Very few people were around, just the hoovering of the cleaning staff. One man behind the desk. The occasional person returning to their room.

I looked around and the masculinity of the wood, the hum of the quiet, and the dark lighting were holding us. Obviously we didn't want to be alone.

"What did you like?" she replied, although I was pretty sure she didn't really care about the answer. No one writes for others really. It is one's own exploration.

"You bring to the surface passion," I said. "You ask, Can desire be allowed to rove free as the winds? You ask because your whole ethos is that love is destructive. Actually Jean believes that too. You both write that love is destructive."

She said nothing. Maybe I was just feeling destructive.

I continued, "Gerhardt said one night that we're all just in love with love. Sometimes the love object gets cancelled out under the weight of this love."

Jean had now come downstairs, too. She stood there on her canes, a string of pearls round her neck. A printed dress. She didn't seem to want to be alone either.

"Let's go for a walk," I said to everyone, "even though it's so late. Let's move," I said. I was so nervous. "Let's just walk." We all agreed, even Jean needed her sticks but, as she had said one evening, "Walking can be a kind of making love. Even at my age."

We had all been silent for a minute, wondering. Till she said, "Whatever age I am," and laughed. And it was true, who knows what age we really are inside?

So we shuffled out of the hotel, the three of us. They with their aging bodies, I with mine that I refused to see as aging, and we walked slowly by the opera house under the moon, by the sculptures of beautiful women that bordered the opera house gardens, so many goddesses and muses, with wide faces and uplifted full breasts, and staring eyes into the centuries ahead of us, by gardens, the trees and grass so softly tended, the night quiet and the light changing everywhere as the hues moved from lamps to stars back to lamps. We walked and sometimes I could hardly go forward, I felt such a wave, for being with these people who were actually with me, who had not abandoned me.

Truth was I was fighting abandoning myself even then by excoriating myself. Why had I so stupidly thought I could do things alone? Why had I not known that it is impossible? My ex had waxed poetic about my independence, calling me a freedom fighter, but here he was now with a woman who was completely dependent on him and he on her.

Why had my mother's rejection and my father's madness set such a tone? Why had I been so sensitive? Had I only trusted writing and words because one could do them, I thought, by oneself? Now I found myself loving working in the theatre, even films, as Marguerite had also done at my age. She made 11 films that she wrote herself. I doubt they made money but she probably, like me, loved the interactivity of working with people, the exchange of energies. I was tired of my own voice alone.

I might have to change my whole life to be with Gerhardt, I realized. I might have to really acknowledge another and let him into my life. I might have to allow him his frailties. I might have to really get to know him and stand by him.

But what could be a better gift than that?

We all sat down on a bench on the Ringstrasse. Marguerite and Jean were tired. They were speaking among themselves, remembering people they knew in common. I turned to Marguerite suddenly and said, "I must go."

"Where?" Jean asked.

"To Gerhardt's."

"You've never even been there," Marguerite said.

"I know."

"Do you know where it is?" Jean asked. "It's 4 in the morning."

I didn't even answer but flipped my phone and called him. He answered sleepily.

"Can I come over?" I asked.

"Is anything wrong?"

"I can't sleep by myself anymore," I said.

"Come over."

I ended the call. I looked at them. "I can't," I said and they nodded as I hailed a taxi.

Ten minutes later, Gerhardt buzzed me in and I climbed some carpeted stairs and he unlocked his apartment door and I entered a room where he had lit one lamp and so I saw the room was full of books and paintings and then I swung my eyes into another room which had no door to it and that room was full of CDs, all so neatly placed.

He was wearing a t-shirt and boxer shorts and he was very tall. Not as athletic in his body as Oskar but cuddly. He took my hand and we passed through those rooms to his bedroom. A white comforter. Windows overlooking a garden. I lay down with him and here I was with a tall man who was suddenly cleaving into my body.

He undid my dress and then he began to kiss me, long kisses, insistent kisses on my breasts. I clung to him as if I was on a life raft and a huge wave was about to come. I almost did not want to make love; I just wanted to be held tightly against the upcoming waves. But he obviously had his own needs and I had interrupted his sleep so I let him move his head down my body and I should not have been surprised at what an oboist would know. And then I took him inside me and his hands knew precisely where to be, as he kissed me and it had been years since I was kissed and I had forgotten that kissing is erotic, and he was enormously tender and enormously giving and enormously sure as he moved symphonically in and on my body.

After, I lay still beside him kissing his neck, I said, " *'He's torn off the dress, he throws it down. He's torn off her little white cotton panties and . . .'* "

"But I see you don't wear underwear," he said smiling.

"Never did," I said. Then I continued, "'. . . and he carries her over like that, naked, to the bed. And there he turns away and weeps. And she, slow, patient, draws him to her and starts to undress him. With her eyes shut. Slowly. He makes as if to help her. She tells him to keep still. Let me do it. She says she wants to do it. And she does. Undresses him. When she tells him to, he moves his body in the bed, but carefully, gently, as if not to wake her.'"

"From *The Lover?*" he asks. He is lying back gazing off. There is no music playing but I can hear Chopin in him.

I nod. I continue from her book, "'*He talks to me, says he knew right away, when we were crossing the river, that I'd be like this after my first lover, that I'd love love. He says he knows now I'll deceive him and deceive all the men I'm ever with.*'"

"Is that true?" he asks.

"It was true for her. Perhaps, in its way it's true for all us, wouldn't you say?"

He didn't answer and I liked that. I nuzzled into him and thought yes, you're right, I still think about Oskar. But it may not mean anything, Gerhardt. I don't know what it means.

And then he turned and put his arms strongly around me, and said, "It was a wonderful thing your calling me like that. I knew to wait till when you wanted."

I nuzzled in. That wave was still out there.

He held me and said; "Now we can listen to a melody."

And I smiled, a bit in a grimace; it was so simple, and so strange to have someone be loving to me. I wasn't used to it and was not sure I could meet it. Who is this man? But I didn't run out of there, I didn't say something distantly hostile, as I could be so adept at. Instead, I smiled and kept my arms around him and just thought, I will try, I will try to be loved this time. I will try to love and see what changes in the world therein.

At least I'll have something new to write about.

TWENTY

The next morning he put me in a taxi to my hotel. I went to my room and thought about all this. I decided that it was good that I had suddenly chosen to begin a new narrative. I took a luxurious bath, washed my hair, put on a white dress and went down to their rooms, feeling that lushness and fullness one has after you have spent a night with someone inside you.

They were up and dressed and talking away. I walked in and it was as if I was interrupting them.

"There is only one subject in writing and it runs as an undercurrent under all other subjects," Marguerite was saying, legs crossed talking to Jean, whom I sat down next to on the flowered eiderdown. Marguerite was sitting on the other bed. They each had a coffee next to them. The light was bright outside since Marguerite had once again opened the heavy drapery to let the sun in. In the distance, on the street, a woman in a black coat and knit hat was walking by the opera house.

"What subject is that?" I asked, jumping up to get a coffee cup from the table and then pouring some coffee for me. I was expecting to hear the requisite sex, desire, power, death subjects.

"There is no mother," she said.

"Funny," I laughed, sitting back down, "many psychiatric schools believe that. There is no mother, meaning we do not get to be taken care of. We have to accept that." I turned to Jean. "What about you? Do you agree?"

Marguerite interrupted me, "Jean was always writing how there was no man. But she meant there was no man acting as the mother to care for her characters. That's why they're always so heart broken, submissive, lost. There is no mother."

"Hmm," I said. I sipped my coffee. Coffee can be a bit of a mother. "Some people write about their cultural experience . . ." I began—

"It's still the longing, the longing for acceptance, love. You," Marguerite said very definitively pointing at me, "don't write as freely as fully as gaily as you should because you need to internalize a good mother who wants to hear from you. Who makes you feel what you have to say is important? A source of joy. Who is happy to let you play?"

I felt a nervousness in my chest as I listened. I wanted to argue but couldn't.

"Plenty of people," I said, "didn't have mothers and were great writers . . . Anyway I thought anguish and isolation were the ultimate creative midwives."

"But it is the pure raw anguish of the child they're talking about," Marguerite said. "In other words, there's something inside that is healing, moving toward the mother, when one is writing."

Marguerite became very intent as if she was following a thread that she was just now unspooling. "For example, as you know, my mother never understood me. She wanted me to help the family get money and I think she admired me but really her life was her sons. I was the more intelligent and the more ambitious, but, for her, it was boys. Liquor was my mother. We all know that. And of course writing."

I turned to Jean. "You?"

She pressed down on her skirt. "My mother also was not the least bit interested in me . . . My father paid a bit of attention. Then he died. Off I went to England to school. Horrible. No wonder I wrote *Wide Sargasso Sea*. I was not only Mrs. Rochester, I was Jane Eyre. I was never really accepted. So school was a nightmare. Then the acting. I wanted men to be my mother, that's true, and really some were. My second husband. Max, my third, tried to be, even my first did, but those two were looking for mothers themselves. I suppose writing was. And booze. Oui, Marguerite, c'est vrai."

I sighed.

Marguerite lifted her eyebrows and said, "We know. We know about you." Again she was pointing at me. "You had no one. Booze a bit. But you never liked drink as much as we did."

"I don't know if I did or didn't," I said. "But I do know I never really let a man be my mother. Or anything I suppose."

"Well you certainly didn't choose very attentive lovers," Jean said. "A lover should be passionate, all over you."

"Maybe it is a mother thing," I said. "We think we want a man to be adoring and indulgent, like a supposed good mother. But do we?"

"Or you mean you wouldn't know what to do if a man was like that," Jean said. "Perhaps, you get hooked on the rejection. That is the familiar mother for you. As far as you'll go toward intimacy.

"Anyway we're here now," Jean said. "Which means this all might change. You may grow to feel rejection is not the type of love you want. And that goes for writing, too. You may not want to be rejected there anymore either."

"Are you both saying we are all just looking for the mother? That's what our lives are?" I asked. "You mean everyone looking for God, which you will notice dear ladies, I have not asked you about, YET, are really looking for their fantasy mothers. Someone to talk to them and take care of them and love them. You mean we need to internalize those feelings, ourselves, in order to act, love or write?"

Marguerite returned, "Isn't this obvious?"

"Yes," I said. "It is . . . but what the hell does it mean?"

"What?" Marguerite asked.

"How does it manifest?"

"You assume the world cares about you. You make contact with it, even if you are frightened. Because deep down you know something good could happen. You don't assume you will be rejected."

"Writers are always rejected."

"But you have to try."

"Yes."

"Same with love," Jean said. "You have to be willing to love and trust in that love."

Here we go again, I thought. "What if the man isn't loving?" I asked.

"You be loving. That is what is important. Anyway, Gerhardt is loving," Jean added.

"She's not talking about Gerhardt," Marguerite said.

"No."

"Don't make any demands of Oskar," Marguerite said. "He is not capable. Be loving if you must and then, if he cannot reciprocate at all, the hell with it. Life is not starvation."

"And Gerhardt?"

"Find out what it feels like to be with someone nice to you."

"I am doing that with you."

"Well it's about bloody time," Jean said.

TWENTY-ONE

I was very proud of myself because I had chosen to take a bus alone to a restaurant where I was to meet Gerhardt. As we sped along through the unfamiliar grand and orderly streets, I talked with a jewelry importer from Bali, a wonderfully mannered and graceful man who spoke English and related his cash flow problems with humility. He worked hard and did his best. He tried to treat his people well, he told me.

That night at another cozy, quiet cream and maroon colored restaurant, Gerhardt seemed a bit tired although his face looked disarmingly young to me and I studied it to see why, and it was because it was full of emotion. He showed his tiredness from the music and the constant rehearsals and perhaps from living alone and then I thought that is beauty, to let your face show its vulnerability. This study I am making.

But also, it turned out when I questioned him, that his face was tired from a girlfriend whom he had recently hurt by leaving her, and apparently she had showed up unannounced at rehearsal and left artwork of his that she had, left it with the man at the door, but she had added her own blood to it. Was she Italian I wondered? Seemed a little operatic. Or was it the Vienna that Egon Schiele had been painting? Gerhardt's face might also have been tired from his childhood poverty, I thought, a father whom he told me had thrown knives at him after he'd had a bit of schnapps, tired from a mother who was timid and broken. Music saved Gerhardt. He was tired from how women had loved him and how much he had to give back. But he, unlike Oskar, kept trying.

At dinner, he and I both ordered hummus, baba ganoush, tabouleh, since it turned out this restaurant was Mediterranean. Gerhardt sat up unusually tall and I once again wondered about his family in the war. Was he a Günter Grass hiding his Nazi past under his extreme sensitivity? Obviously his family was unglued enough to have been attracted to the rigidity of Nazism. My own grandmother and mother had been in Vienna at that time and they both escaped but not the rest of their family. But was it really any of my business about his family in the war? The war was over sixty years ago. And I have often mulled over how brave I would have been. I have my doubts. Would I have fought the prevailing government? I have never succumbed to anything. But I would not have been brave. I would have moved, as my own family did. I have always chosen flight over fight. And that's why I've been alone.

So many great artists were killed and Gerhardt is intelligent enough to know this, all that genius that was in Vienna and Berlin. Prague. I was not so caring about French genius and what happened to them since Oskar's girlfriends are always French. French and young.

I didn't think it was appropriate to bring up the issue of who was a Nazi and who was not, even if we were in a restaurant near the Jacobplatz. I did it a different way.

"You know," I said, "there are these new German orchestras playing only Jewish music so as to re-integrate it into German culture. The government and Jewish communities are funding them. So it's like a new renaissance of Jewish music in Germany. A step away from the war . . ."

"Yes, I know about them, Orchestra Jacobplatz." I was a little shocked at the synchronicity.

Then I heard him say . . . "Marguerite was involved with a German in the war. You know that, yes?"

I nodded. "She never speaks about it. Mostly because I guess from her perspective everyone—German and French—ended up in the same place, which is to say, dead. But yes. She claimed she was helping the resistance and indeed I think she set him up to be shot by her resistance pals while Marguerite and the German were having lunch. But the hit never came off. But she testified against him after the war. He was shot anyway."

"Do you think they were lovers?" Gerhardt asked. "Biographies are vague about it, as was she in *The War*."

"Her lover, Dionys Mascolo, once described either *The War* or *The Lover*, I forget, as a cruel terrible work," I said. "He was echoing a phrase of Rimbaud. Dionys said this because he believed she wrote in such a way that did not involve making the book say more but rather drawing from it what it could not say. I don't know if that answers your question."

He said nothing. I don't think he followed me.

So I began again, "I think she enjoyed the flirtation. Women enjoy flirtations. I think the German was quite taken with her. But he never did really help her, which I think he promised. To find information on Robert, that was her husband. I think the German told her he would protect Robert but he didn't. That," I said, "is probably what she hated him for. Along with the ideologies and what was going on with everyone."

"But do you think they had an affair?" He had ordered another beer. Austrian.

"I could ask her. Marguerite liked to drink. Maybe boundaries got a bit fuzzy with booze. I don't know. She is a principled woman—I don't think she did."

"But Mitterrand thought maybe—"

"I know. She and the German had those lunches, etc. . . . she was acting as a lure and when you are a lure you can get into the part . . ."

"Are you speaking from experience?" he smiled.

"Yes," I said, "and no. I think when I slept with men whom I did business with, I did not care for those men, but I did sleep with them. I don't know. I was so hungry for attention when I was young. I wanted to be held, all the time. I was always looking for someone to save me . . ."

"Why are you crying?" he asked. He was looking so intently, so caringly at me.

"I don't think I've changed much," I said.

The waiter placed our dishes in front of us and looked disdainfully down at me as he set the plates in front of us. The Austrians don't believe in unabashed shows of emotion. My mother never did either. Except her own.

I was drinking water with my dinner. And here I am with water, acting drunk. These good mothers were intoxicating me, unraveling my feelings. They were affecting me.

I loved Gerhardt right now because I could talk to him.

He took my hand. "That is understandable," he said. "Marguerite does not like me," he added, "Maybe because I am Austrian."

"She likes you," I lied. "She thinks the distance will do us in."

But the truth was for some reason she preferred Oskar. She liked Oskar's quick wit and indirect ways of expressing himself, which is a bit like art. She was not impressed with Gerhardt's sensitive feelings. She liked Oskar's consistency and strong sense of self. On the other hand, it didn't bother her that I never heard from Oskar. He must be busy with the redhead's heart. Or maybe he does not think about hearts at all.

As I sat at dinner, my own heart began to ache a bit. Age and creativity and aloneness and a world I did not understand. I had always focused on the internal landscape as if that would guide me in the world and now I knew that it doesn't. It's got nothing to do with what is outside, no matter what the new age books are saying. There is no law of attraction. Nietzsche had it right. People are driven by a desire to feel better than the other. I took my other hand and reached for Gerhardt.

It had been long enough that I had held Oskar and been left alone.

"I must learn German," I said.

And Gerhardt gave the most romantic answer, he could. He leveled his eyes at me and smiled, "Indeed, you must."

TWENTY-TWO

Nobody talked about leaving Vienna. We just didn't seem to be going home. This hotel bill must be astronomical, I thought. Maybe they have unlimited money in heaven. I hope they didn't decide to get all ethereal on me when it came to paying and leave me the job of settling up. I would end up like Egon Schiele—in an Austrian jail.

I decided to take a walk and I was standing outside the doctor's office. My face was normal now, so I was no longer averse to the vicinity. I was just standing there, like a homing pigeon, wondering where to fly next. A tall, older good looking man, about sixty, well-dressed and self-assured, came out of the bookstore, carrying a package, and gave me a cursory look. If I were thirty years younger, he would have smiled. I was brooding about this when I heard, "Are you American?"

It was he, the philanthropist, whom Jean had seen at Beethoven's *Missa Solemnis*. The one I had written about in my room. Here he was in a grey sweater, cashmere slacks. Lovely long grey hair, which curled up around his neck. Patrician nose. Grey blue piercing eyes. I took this all in at once while he asked me if I am American. Marguerite had put it well in *The Lover*: "*He lit a cigarette and gave it to me. And very quietly, close to my lips, he talked to me. And I talked to him too, very quietly.*

"*Because he doesn't know for himself,*" she wrote, "*I say it for him, in his stead. Because he doesn't know he carries within him a supreme elegance, I say it for him.*"

I nodded to the philanthropist. What did he want? Directions? Why would he ask an American for directions?

"Are you on holiday?" he asked, assertively.

I nodded again, sizing him up. "Well," I said. "I'm not sure."

He squinted at me. "Care to come to the museum with me?"

I did a double take. How long since someone had invited me anywhere extemporaneously?

"You remind me of the painter Mercedes Matter," he said. "You're vivid like her."

I nodded yet again and began to lope alongside him. I didn't make conversation. I didn't know what to say.

We walked into the museum and immediately the staff began bowing and scraping, without asking us to pay, I suppose because he probably had funded one of the wings, and he said, "Let's go see Cezanne's card players."

"Okay."

"What I like is they are regular people, holding their cards," he said, gently moving me so that I went first through the doorway into the paintings salon. I always like the way a man gently moves you, positions you to go before him, as if it is politesse, which I suppose it is. "They're holding the cards they've been given and they're living with them, not playing them."

I got the metaphor.

We walked round the clean white rooms in the museum where Cezanne's many drawings were hanging, the ones he did to prepare for the paintings and the beauty of the paintings. Cezanne had written that he never wanted to leave his home, there was so much for him to paint, everything he needed to paint was in his town.

I was beginning to feel that way about Vienna.

"I saw you at a concert," I said.

"The Israeli Philharmonic?"

"Yes."

"I made a big point of officiating there," he said, his eyes on the paintings, "to show these Viennese what's what. I'm amazed they allowed the Israelis to play."

"The war is over," I said.

"As far as the Jews are concerned," he said, "the war is never over. You look Jewish," he said.

I was surprised because I didn't think I did. Small turned up nose.

"My mother was a Viennese Jew."

"What was her name?" he asked.

Was my fantasy going to come true? Are we related? "Daisy Steiner."

"Hmmm," he said. "I wonder if anyone knew her."

"I know I didn't," I said smiling.

"Women are like that. Very tricky."

"As if men aren't!" I said.

"True."

We had finished our spin through the museum. All those paintings, sculptures, the design of the museum itself, the artistry of the displays—all that creative energy was erotic. I always feel aroused in a museum. I looked at him and, all of a sudden, I was on fire. I hoped it was not embarrassing, as if I was after him. But I knew that my hair was fuller, my eyes were flashing, my heart pounding, my mouth more intent.

"Well," he said, taking my hand, "this was most pleasant. I am sure we will see each other again. Vienna is in reality a small town."

"I hope so," I said. And I did. He was lovely to be with, steady, sure of himself, full of life.

Suddenly I remembered Jean saying at one of our dinners that she always longed for someone entirely secure, yet entirely sensitive, someone utterly respectable and safe, yet able to understand her lonely, fearful, rebellious nature. Against all expectations, her first British lover really had been this dream. But his respectability rejected her, as she'd been afraid it would—and so did the very things that drew him to her, his own hidden loneliness and fear. "As soon as he felt the real depths of my need," she said, "he must have wanted to bolt."

My mind returned to where I was standing just as the philanthropist bowed and strolled out.

We had not even asked each other one another's names.

I ambled slowly about the museum, confused. Some Da Vinci drawings that were not as sensual as they were purported to be and then I went messily, excited, alive, desirous in my heart, back to the hotel.

Jean and Marguerite had told me not to bother them. They were busy writing.

TWENTY-THREE

The next week I hardly saw them at all. All of us quieted down and were not interacting. In the morning I went to the breakfast room with my computer and wrote as I sipped my coffees and had some bread and cheese from the hotel buffet, and I wrote about a young girl, who finally had come to me, this young girl who had no one. No one at all. But she was driven to not suffer her loneliness. She was plucky, defiant, insistent. She went out on Halloween, dressed as Eliza Doolittle, on the wrong night but went out she did, because that was the night she thought it was and the only night she could get away from her Bulgarian guardian who knew nothing of Halloween nor wanted to. Her guardian, like the girl, had lost everyone and was a shut in, choosing to eschew her own life in deference to those who had lost theirs. The guardian had taken this girl in for the money. But the money was not going to pay; she made clear to the girl, for any rustling up of feelings towards the girl in her heart.

Our young girl also insisted on having herself bat mitzvahed, even without family, since her own had abandoned her because, once they lost all their own family, murdered in that war, they could not live with the grief of all those who had been taken away from them, so they left our young girl, as they had been left, and when the other bah mitzvah children were joined on the bema in the synagogue by proud grandparents and parents and siblings, my young girl stood alone, small dark, brave, remarkably like myself. The rabbi had been kind to her, and the girl smiled in response, but she was not fooled, she knew her destiny.

I wrote about her and she aged on my pages, publishing work eventually, writing about those who have no one—in other words in some ways all of us—she lived her life, a hard life since she made a living by living in her mind, not living in commerce. Her intimacy was with music which soothed her as a mother should, and she loved men when she got older, most of them abandoned characters themselves, and they did not give her much, but some attention, nor did she have children, because children reminded her of sadness, but hers was a brave existence and after breakfast I went back to my room, worked on it some more, then went for a walk in Vienna, again along a *strasse* under the trees to the Weiner Musicverein and back, always the same route or through the gardens with the stiff Austrian men with their canes and dogs, both of whom were unfriendly, to look at Beethoven's statue, or to see the Brueghel paintings, and then back to my room to rewrite what I wrote.

I didn't see my two friends. How long? Had they gone to Budapest, which Jean thought even lovelier than Vienna? I did not think they were unkind and wherever they were, they would return to at least say goodbye. I didn't think they would leave me like that girl in my story had been left. Both these women had been left so much in their own lifetimes; they wouldn't inflict that on me. I knew they would resurface. I knew the knowledge of death had made them kind, no matter what they had been like when they were alive the first time.

At night I had dinner in small restaurants with Gerhardt before he went to play, and then I came back to my hotel and rewrote more. Sometimes I went to hear him, Janacek, Poulenc, others, and it was exciting, both the music and seeing him up there but I only went when it was the music program itself that called me. I didn't go any old time. That's because I would see Gerhardt anyway. After a concert that I did not attend, he would pick me up and I would go to bed with him. Make love with him in the exquisite tender way he had and sleep curled very close to him and wake up to find my fingers entwined in his.

And I didn't realize that this went on for weeks.

TWENTY-FOUR

Jean and I were sitting at breakfast. Dishes and waiters were moving all around us. She widened her lit blue eyes at me and pronounced, "At least we don't have to go to the expense or time of mailing your manuscript out from Vienna. Saves a lot of money, email."

Then Marguerite walked officiously into the dining room with the manuscript. I had asked her to read it. Can you imagine having these two women read your work? One's idols of literature. Only a fool, etc. . . .

Marguerite sat down in her beige sweater set that did not hide her plump waist, a brown pencil skirt and ordered coffee and then turned to me, "It's good," she said, in the voice of a teacher to a pupil she might have been doubtful about. "You should send it out."

"There's one thing I don't like about it," Jean said.

"What?"

"It sounds a little like us."

I laughed. "What do you mean?"

"The loneliness does," she responded. "The character lives in it."

"We all do," Marguerite said. "There is no escape from that. That is what in a way everyone is writing. Or at least in serious work they are."

"Not Shakespeare," I said, to be contradictory.

"Plays are different," Marguerite said. "Everyone is interacting. That is the thing, as they say. But in novels, one goes into . . . that existential longing."

I looked around the room for a second, looking for anyone, anyone that might make contact with me, and then said, "Well, if I write like you in any sort of way, it would be quite a compliment."

"Well you have to have that belief, dear. You have to," Jean said. "Anyway what does it matter? Ford always advised me and encouraged me, it's true. He told me to read the French classical writers, and to write about what I knew. And when his advice agreed with my instincts as a writer, I followed it, otherwise, I didn't."

Then she turned to Marguerite. "Let's go out and have a drink and meet some men."

"Alright," she said. "I like that bar down the street in the Royal Hotel." Then she turned to me, "You should be able to entertain yourself by now."

I nodded, "I should. Be home before midnight."

Jean laughed, "Hopefully not, darling."

It seems we were all rather peaceful right now, just being who we are.

And the funny part was that was the exact change that all of us needed or came to effect. Just to be who we are.

TWENTY-FIVE

When Gerhardt came to get me, we would walk to his small apartment that overlooked his street of immaculately tended two floor houses and gardens with neat rows of hydrangeas and roses and flavia flowers, which he said you can get high on, bees do, or someone does, maybe people I forget and then I remembered Oskar telling me that elephants have a favorite vine that they like to eat that gets them drunk.

"Do they start sleeping with other elephant's wives and stuff?"

"Yes," he said, after some tennis game, "they like this vine when they want to have a party."

At Gerhardt's apartment, I fixated on how he had photographs hung everywhere of people laughing, women in doorways, even cadavers laughing and that was how I knew he must be sad. His furniture was thin and modern, not really warm, a man's apartment. No carpets. He would pour me a red wine and we'd talk. About his friends. About his work. About mine. I just loved listening to his deep, heavily accented voice. Then we would go to bed. And he would kiss me, slowly. And soon he would be inside me and it was so erotic, since he was creative with my body, as if it was a marvelous work of art itself, one he must have to live, and my whole body had changed from the separate body that I had had with Oskar, one that he never touched, one that was there somehow to give him an orgasm and then sleep, but not one to be cherished. My body had changed into one that was connected to Gerhardt's.

But when Gerhardt spoke so seriously and lovingly to me, the next morning, of an upcoming appointment I was scheduled for with a dentist, I would think, Oskar wouldn't bother with this minutia.

"This is not so important," I said to Gerhardt.

"Tiny details," he replied didactically, "is the stuff of love."

When Gerhardt told me that he had a great sense of humor, my heart fell further, since no one with a great sense of humor would obviously ever mention it. There was no question I loved his treating me well, and I loved that he could discuss his feelings, or rather, he did not dismiss mine. But as I listened to him stiffly complain how the oboist, Wilhelm, next to him missed his notes, or how the American guest conductor was always too easy on the musicians, I felt suffocated by the constant droning pettiness. The complaints themselves were not annoying; it was the lack of joy when he spoke.

I didn't show it though. I nodded my head feigning interest while I was recalling Jean telling me that she and her second husband, Leslie, had what she called a 50-50 affair, everything was even, proper, without passion. Passionate love affairs were 100-100. If they were 1000-1000, then you knew you would get scorched. Soon Jean and Leslie were living together, and finally they married. They liked each other, she said, but they weren't in love. Leslie was not as rich or as well connected as the man Jean had loved (Lancelot), just as Gerhardt was not as rich or as sure of himself as Oskar. Leslie, Jean's 50-50 husband, was well educated and well spoken, kind and chivalrous, reserved and self-controlled. In many ways he combined for Jean the best qualities of her other English gentlemen: Lancelot's kindness and sense of honor and Ford's care for her writing. But she and Leslie were not in love.

And I was seeing that I was not in love with Gerhardt.

Gerhardt was still talking about how important it was to tell each other everything in love. I wasn't sure, since I was so content by myself in my own mind.

After breakfast with Gerhardt, I went back to the hotel to write or meet with my friends. Marguerite was still daunted that we were not having success with my novel. It was confounding to her. She had published a lot during her life. Made many films. She worked with Jeanne Moreau and other actors. None of her films, except *Hiroshima, Mon Amour* which Alain Resnais directed were that successful. Resnais knew how to work with her. Just write, he said, write the scenes. I'll take care of the rest.

She had a reputation, but it was mostly with intellectuals, like herself. It was *The Lover*, which she wrote fairly quickly, in her house by the sea that put her on the map. Before that she had some success, but in *The Lover* she held nothing back, even though the book is very slim. She wrote what it was to be a writer, to have been a girl needing money from a man, what it was to have a mother who could be considered to have used her, what it was to have her mother prefer her con-man brother, what it was to love her younger brother, a sweet young boy, who died, what it was to drink. She wrote it quietly but entirely honestly, and the words had the profundity and truth of the sea inside her. She was an instant celebrity.

Some say the rampant success ruined her. She referred to herself in the third person after that. She was on TV shows. She was no longer poor. Although she could no longer attract men, she attracted everyone else. She was an icon.

People, like me, admired her. A certain kind of reader found her too narcissistic. But a writer, a poet, a woman saw how she inferred that once you give yourself away, you never get yourself back, you continue to give yourself away, you watch yourself as you do it, and how she knew this packed a wallop.

Jean had some success in her fifties. Her stories about her own life and the problems she had. Then the books went out of print. Because the stories are sad, they were not well received. Then she began working for 15 years on what happened to Mrs. Rochester, the woman upstairs in Jane Eyre. Why there had to be a fire after a fire in the heart. This book was also about her. How some men love you but cannot sustain it since it requires momentary lapses of forgetting about themselves. How love is tied up with money. Someone marries someone for security, which it seems, in Jean's books and in Marguerite's is never realized. And because it isn't, love is forsaken. *Wide Sargasso Sea* came out when Jean was seventy-six and she made herself up for parties but it was sad, she said, that it had not come earlier. Her husbands were dead. And she was often dead drunk herself. I've already told you much of this. I tell you again because Jean said, "You see, we don't want this to happen to you."

But they didn't realize it had happened to me. It had all happened inside me so what is the difference? Everything they experienced—loss, rejection, need, betrayal—was inside me. As it always is with someone you love and admire.

But the truth was, by embracing them inside me, all those feelings of hurt and victories, theirs and mine, and letting myself be loved by Gerhardt and learning to maybe love him back, while trying to separate from Oskar's unwillingness—it seemed I had never been happier. So they hadn't bought my novel. Big deal. I had written it.

TWENTY-SIX

I decided to move in with Gerhardt. Somewhere in my heart I made that decision the first night I made love with him, even though I hadn't bothered to articulate it to myself. I was tired of being alone and, unlike Oskar, Gerhardt wanted me. I knew I was not to be trusted in love, that I had never been good at yielding. I would learn how to love, I told myself. He lived in Vienna, I lived in New York, but I would stay. It is good to be with another. Making love that first night, I had been shocked to remember what it was when a man touched my breasts, my neck, my face, my body, when a man treated me as worthy of entwining with, when a man put his arms around me with conviction. And I was still in this amazement and somehow felt I always would be. I did not want to choose a life where I was never held.

When Gerhardt read the paper in the morning, he would say, "I must take you to such and such," a place he was reading about. "We must go for a drive to the country. You have never seen the Alps." "On your birthday we'll have dinner in Paris." "You really have never been to Venice? What kind of men have you known? We'll go, we'll go when the music season is finished."

I forgot what it was to be taken to meet relatives and friends as if I was a jewel to be shown off. I forgot what it was to say something and the man takes a key from it. "I am not so fond of Wilde," he said, "but we can go to that play if you like." I forgot what it was to have someone interested in my work and how that helps my own interest in my work. I forgot that to be an artist was not an anathema, and not just the plague of financial ruin, but an exploration and that a man, a man might support me in that. I had forgotten.

Everyday I drew closer to Gerhardt. Each morning, now that I had finished that novel, I took a German lesson and then wrote. Studying and living in another language made me appreciate the sounds of my own language more intimately and my writing once again became sensual and an inner exploration. The Private Lives of Sentences.

I chose to go at night to hear the Philharmonik when they were playing Beethoven or Vaughan Williams or Ravel, and my heart swelled with music and pride, listening to the perfection of the orchestra and knowing that the handsome brilliant oboist was the man I would go home with. After the concert, some of the musicians and Gerhardt and I would have a late dinner at the restaurant with the maroon walls. They'd speak in German and then translate for me some of their jokes about the coughing in the concert hall or when the conductor had lost his place.

Then one would look at me and say, "Are we cold Viennese even nodding yet when we see you on the street?"

"Yesterday the newspaper man made some ironic remark. I could tell by his tone he was acknowledging me although I did not understand what he said. It's a start."

The old small violinist put his hand on my arm. "You'll know you truly belong when you find all of us completely boring."

In the morning, Gerhardt would rehearse at the Musikverein and I would meet him on the Ringstrasse at noon and we would walk since he liked to get some exercise and enjoy the outdoors. We shopped at the Naschmarkt, bought expensive blouses on Kartner Strasse, and candied violets in Demel's Rococo salon. He was always voluble, open, sensitive, and attentive to whatever I had to say. He would thank me for being with him.

It made me profoundly uncomfortable but I thought maybe that was my problem, not his.

Jean and Marguerite were not about, strangely. When I went to the Hotel Sacher, they were never there. I told Gerhardt they had disappeared and he smiled and said probably not for good. "Don't worry, they can take care of themselves. Maybe they are happy, too," he said, and god I wished it was true.

I wanted time to stop. We heard nothing on my novel and this was sad and Gerhardt said, "Work on another one" and of course this was true, also.

Each morning, after rehearsal, he brought back flowers. Gorse for hope. Holly for being wounded or for when I was wounding. Impatiens for staying my hurriedness. Madia to enhance concentration. Mariposa lilies for my lack of mothering, he said. Pink yarrow to help me keep boundaries. I laughed at the perfume of it.

I said to Gerhardt, "Jean once wrote, '*There were two breezes, the sea breeze and the land breeze. People said that they called the land breeze the undertaker breeze. But I never thought that. It smelt of flowers.*'"

He smiled in response and brought a breeze of different flowers into the apartment every day. For me.

TWENTY-SEVEN

I began taking walks back and forth to the Hotel Sacher, in case I saw them. I sat on the benches on the *strasse* in front of the opera house, Weiner Staatsoper. I imagined Gustav and Alma moving about here, Gustav with his legendary limping speed walk. I felt like I was missing my own family.

The Viennese artists, so many of them . . . who were here in the '10s and '20s, all the writers, all those minds of fury drifting around on the streets and cafes, and now in my mind.

My own grandparents. Where are they all? Dead. And even my new adopted family—of these two women writers—have now become scarce.

I pulled a volume of poetry out of my pocket. Charles Olson. And it reminded me of great writing in our own time, continual minds of fury.

I looked around at this strange city I had landed myself in. And then I saw Oskar watching me from the bench across the path. Check pants. Green shirt. Green tie. This man of many colors. Who at times felt all knowing to me.

He tipped his brown felt hat. His sharp brown eyes already had a shine of victory about them.

"What are you doing here?" I asked.

"I could ask the same of you."

"I live here."

At this point, neither of us had moved, each on our own bench. We were sparring, but truth is we both like to spar. It's the Maccabean blood.

"Why do you live here?" he asked.

"I told you a thousand times I wanted a partner. I had to go to another continent to find one."

"You were precipitous."

I looked at him. I remembered Jean saying Rochester was not really a heel. "As soon as I saw that it all came to life," she explained. "It had always been there . . . Mr. Rochester is not a heel. He is a fierce and violent man who marries an alien creature, partly because his father arranges it, partly because he has had a bad attack of fever, partly no doubt for lovely mun, but most of all because he is curious about this girl – already half in love. Then . . . they get to this lovely lonely magic place and there is no 'half' at all."

"I don't want to be half loved," I said to Oskar.

He ignored me, taking me in very closely with his eyes. He stayed fast on his bench which, yes, the green paint matched his clothes. "You have your normal face back, I see."

"Yes."

"Don't you miss me?" he asked.

I looked over at him with a bit of a grimace. "You know Duras in *Emily L.* wrote it perfectly."

"Wrote what?" he asked.

"She wrote, '*You say it's also because she loved the Captain so much that she sometimes wanted to leave him.*'"

"I don't get it," he responded. But I knew he was lying. Not getting things was never his problem.

What he meant was he refused to get it. But he knew, he knew I did miss him. But why did I? I wondered.

"Maybe you're the quintessential American," I said to him. "Positive. Commercial. Maybe I miss that a bit since I was breast fed on images of it . . . I miss that you make me laugh, Oskar, but as I told you I like someone loving me and letting me love him." Was I trying to convince myself? "So that is why I literally moved away."

He said nothing till finally I heard, "I don't believe you."

"Why are you here? I don't get it." I now moved to his bench. He had always known I would be the one to move. His body was a gravitational pull for me.

He was smiling too. "To bring you back."

And it was then, out of the corner of my eye, I saw Marguerite and Jean walking to their hotel. I wanted to run to them but I thought, stay and finish this conversation, as useless as it's going to be.

"Bring me back to what?" I asked. "God forbid that we have any vulnerability because it might lead to problems, right?"

He didn't know what to say. He had expected me to fold easily. I always used to.

"I'm staying here Oskar because I want to work on my own work. You don't respect me as an artist. You think it's a joke. You think everything is a joke—"

"Everything IS a joke," he said, "since we are all so inconsequential. We'll be dead shortly."

"That's true. But not inconsequential."

And I looked over at Jean and Marguerite walking. Not inconsequential at all.

"If I think everything's a joke, why am I here?"

Marguerite and Jean had seen me and were walking over slowly toward us.

"Who's that with Jean?" he asked.

"Marguerite Duras."

"Yes and I'm the King of England."

I looked at him because sometimes I think he DID think he was the King of England.

They came over and I said, "Where have you been?"

"Writing," Jean said. "You can't be hanging about with old women all the time."

Duras said to Oskar, "What are you doing here?"

"Why? Where should I be?" he answered quickly.

Jean said, "But what ARE you doing here?"

"I came to see her," he responded.

"Why?" Jean asked.

He sat up and he said the first honest words I had ever heard out of his mouth, "I don't know."

But I did know. He had had a chance with me. Of a real life. And part of him wanted that and part of him didn't.

"Oskar," I said, "I am old and poor."

"Why do you say such unkind things to yourself?" he asked.

I looked at him confused.

Marguerite said, "I am always telling her that, too."

"I was just trying to give you the freedom to be your independent self," he said. "You don't want a normal relationship. You would be bored and hate it."

I had been worried about the same. I wasn't doing well with Gerhardt. I did find it all a bit cloying.

"One can be loving," I tried, "and give a person the freedom to be themselves without leaving them alone all the time."

"But you need to be alone," he said. "You're an artist."

"What rubbish," Marguerite and Jean said.

Marguerite said, "Picasso's last words to his doctor were: 'It's good to have a wife.'"

"I didn't need to be alone," I said. "You did."

"Well," he said, getting up finally, "let's take a weekend in the Alps together and we can discuss this civilly. Book something in St. Moritz."

And then he walked jauntily off in his green pants.

I looked helplessly at Marguerite and Jean.

Where had Gerhardt gone in my mind? It was as if I had been waiting for Oskar to come to his senses all along.

"We'll be on the benches near the hotel," Jean said. "Take a bit of a stroll to cool off."

"It's such a bloody problem," I said, and then I kissed them both.

Jean said, "Do you mind if I borrow your watch?"

"My watch?" It wasn't expensive but it was an odd request.

I took it off and gave it to her, thinking I felt strange giving someone dead a belonging. But god knows the economy worked on dead people giving live people their belongings.

Jean was clasping it and then I waved to them both. "See you shortly," and then I began walking, as usual, in circles.

TWENTY-EIGHT

In actuality, once I walked toward the Musikverein and back, I changed direction again, and began walking toward Gerhardt's and there was Jean and Marguerite now sitting near the hotel on benches in the sun, talking to two older men I didn't know. One had shaved his head to get rid of the grey. The other had straggly blonde hair, that kind of blonde that one doesn't know if it is grey or will never go grey. Both men were smiling, dressed in casual shirts that caught the light, their black sneakers peering up at the sun, and you could feel the heat of their energy.

I walked over. The two women were brimming.

Jean had moved her skirt to be a bit shorter and was kicking her varicosed vein leg. Duras had a pursed smile and her hair seemed to be moving a bit in the breeze. Their old faces looked young with joy and hope.

They introduced me to the men and said they had known them before. In fact, they had all agreed to go for the weekend to an Inn in Salzburg that was old-fashioned, they said, but beautiful and the food and waters were worth going back to. They would have a good time, they said. And Marguerite had a gleam in her eye.

They were going, they said, so they could talk and be together. Remember old times; see if there is such a thing as new ones. "Or are we only always recreating old ones anyway?" Marguerite asked one of the men.

I gave them a look.

I was instantly jealous that they were going on an adventure although I could have asked Gerhardt to go on one. Or I could in fact go with Oskar to St Moritz.

Jean looked at me and saw my despondency. "Stay with Gerhardt," she said. "Don't get sucked back in by Oskar's unavailability."

I nodded, sad that I was so transparent.

"You don't want to starve," Marguerite said. "He's just luring you back in for the fun of it. He has no intention of actually being there. He doesn't know how."

"I thought you liked Oskar," I said to Marguerite.

"I do, but he wants safety in love. This I cannot forgive. I saw it today when I met him."

The two men began complimenting the women.

Jean replied, "I never could do anything—maybe that is why I was unsuccessful with men."

"You offered wit," one said. "That's not offering nothing. And your laugh."

"Wit," she laughed. "I wonder how much of a premium on that . . ." and now they were all going out to have a drink at a café.

I was happy seeing them joyous and busy in their own lives, happy to see they were letting me go. "See you later," I said, glad that I was walking to Gerhardt's. I hoped he was there, but we might have crossed paths when he left for the Musikverein.

"Gerhardt?" I called out, once I had turned the lock.

The lights were switched off. No answer. He must be at the concert hall.

No note from him but that was not unusual.

I sat down and thought. Here I am. In this home. Safe. Loved. With a man of music. What I had always wanted. In a beautiful city. In a new language that makes my own clearer. Why am I feeling despondent? Because Oskar of the electric energy is painting a cardboard picture for me? Why is he here, though? He is making some kind of an effort, even if it doesn't make sense.

I looked over at the table and there was a little antique bottle Oskar had given me that I had brought with me from the States, with bits of shiny confetti in it, that was called *Dream Dust*, "guards against nightmares and helps make dreams come true." Why had he given me that? To make me fool myself into thinking that he might love me one day?

Was he here to make his own dreams come true? What were they? I had never asked. Mine had always been so clamoring, visceral, obvious.

What were his? And was I despondent because I could feel his sadness, his insecurity. He was lost. He wanted his dreams to come true, too, whatever they were.

And then I grew frightened of how my mind could go off on its own sailing course that usually had little to do with reality.

I called Oskar on his cell phone and I said, "Do you love me?"

"Yes," he said. "But I am not in love with you."

I listened.

"You're immensely important to me," he said. "Immensely. That's why I am here."

"Do you mean we don't have a future?"

"I didn't say that."

"You didn't say anything."

"Right," he said.

"You mean you just want to know I am there, here," I said.

"Right," he said. "I don't like change. You were there. You should stay there."

"A fixed object for your fixity."

"Right."

"No waves on my part."

"Preferably."

"I'll get back to you."

"You're wonderful," he said.

And then, just as confused as I always had been, I put the phone down. And I remembered something else Jean wrote, *"'You are a damn hard man for a young man.'"*

"'So you say, so you say.'

"'I tell her so. I warn her. I say this is not a man who will help you when he sees you break up. Only the best can do that. The best—and sometimes the worst.'

"'But you think I'm one of the worst, surely?'

"'No, she said indifferently, to me you are not the best, nor the worst. You are—she shrugged—you will not help her. I tell her so.'"

TWENTY-NINE

I slumped my way over to the hotel the next morning. They were both there. I called from the lobby and asked if we could meet. Marguerite said we should all come to her room.

"I dreamed last night that Oskar would never marry me," I said, staring at the open curtained window. "I asked him why and he said, Money. I said, You could get a prenup in your favor but this did not dissuade him. There was a circus of people around him. He was with me, he said, but he would never commit."

"What is new about that?" Marguerite was reading the newspaper as she said this.

"Maybe Oskar is you," Jean said. "You have the circle of people around you. And it is his money that keeps you away."

I ignored her and continued. "The night before I dreamed that Oskar went off with a young woman in front of me. I felt humiliated. A bear was trying to break into the room I was in with him. Finally the bear roared in and it was just an over-dressed woman," I said.

"Oskar connects with the young woman in you, the more passive part of you. The bear breaking in," Marguerite said, "is the more furious part of you, the woman."

Suddenly Jean laughed.

"What are you laughing at?" I asked.

"I remember this," she said. And then she began acting from *Wide Sargasso Sea*. "*'Your wife!' she said. 'You make me laugh. I don't know all you did but I know some. Everybody knows that you marry her for her money and you take it all. And then you want to break her up, because you jealous of her. She is more better than you, she have better blood in her and she don't care for money—It's nothing for her. Oh I see that first time I look at you. You young but you already hard. You fool the girl. You make her think you can't see the sun for looking at her.'*"

"He never looked at me that way, believe me," I said. Maybe a few times, I mildly recalled, one Christmas day at a small old-fashioned restaurant on 9th Street. He had been so happy to be in that Rococo room with a fire and me being so adoring. Who wouldn't I feel a bit exhilarated by that kind of unceasing attention?

Duras said, "Knowing you, you wouldn't notice if he had been taken with you. You don't notice things like that. You can't tell when someone loves you, so sure are you that they don't."

"What is wrong with Gerhardt?" Jean asked.

"Absolutely nothing," I said. "Absolutely nothing at all."

"So there you are," Jean said. "And now that someone who only wants a part of you is out of your life, you will have more of you. More of you for your work. And more of you to love. And more of a man to love."

"Yes."

"You will have the self respect of someone who wants intimacy."

"Yes." But I remembered all the lovely dinners Oskar's chef cooked for us. The fires he had waiting. But then he had those for himself anyway.

"Gerhardt is—" I said.

"No he isn't. He loves you. You're just not used to that. Gerhardt likes to do things together. He shows you pictures of himself, his family, his friends. He wants to know about your life. Calls. Listens. Your own mother or father never did that so you find it cloying."

"Yes."

"He is not frightened of your poverty since he sees you as wealth itself. And anyway he is not frightened of poverty because he is too busy living a life of art. There is no poverty with that. Some inconvenience, but not poverty."

"Yes."

"He even thinks you're beautiful," Marguerite said. "Because he has the wherewithal to look inside a person, not at them superficially. He is not a fool . . ."

"Yes."

"So with that in mind, you just keep finding jobs," Jean said. "There is no indignity in that. Anyway maybe one of your books will sell. Maybe not. But you keep going on. It's in the nature of life. It's a river and there is movement, unless one steps out. And you are not the type to step out."

We all were silent.

"Oskar doesn't like women," Marguerite said. "It's not unusual but it's obvious. He is frightened of feeling. But it will hit him at some point. You're not the woman to do it because your values are not his. If he meets a woman with money or sheen, that will mesmerize him, as Gerhardt's artistry and sensitivity have mesmerized you and yours has mesmerized him."

"Yes." But I wanted to have that sheen, didn't they know?

"You just like the sheen," Jean answered, "because it compensates for how meager you feel inside. But it's an illusion, darling. The sheen is just sheen. You are so much more than that. So be it."

"Yes."

Jean got up on her sticks and then whooshed me with one of them. "This is love, darling. You have love in your life. What you always wanted. A handsome, loving, good man. He's got flaws but one of them isn't apathy toward you. He is not frightened to love. Don't you be. Do you have any idea how far we came to tell you this?"

THIRTY

Gerhardt was on the road with the Philharmonik. They were playing in Holland. I was alone which may not have been such a bad thing as I tried so hard to understand, understand the woman who held on so tight that happiness couldn't break in the door. I walked around the city, in the summer heat, with my head down, avoiding people's eyes. Over what, you ask? That here I was, pondering the responsibilities of love, mine and another's, and it had taken till nearly sixty to do so. I knew in my heart I could not offer a man prettiness or potential anymore. I could not go to school and study Arabic and begin a bright new career. I could not take a very long running chance. I could only offer what was left of my life, me. Funny, imaginative, loving, defiant and worn me.

"Well hello again."

I was by the museum. It was the philanthropist.

"Why so glum?" he asked, motioning to a bench on the roof that overlooked the city and the museum gardens. We walked together through Palace flowerbeds and Venuses leaning over us as if we did this every day. Sculptures of heroes and gods surrounded us.

We sat down together as if we lived here, at the museum. He crossed his handsome long legs, and stared at me curiously. Why was he now popping up everywhere? I felt held in his steady gaze. What did I have to lose anymore? I should see what cards he wanted us to play. Actually life, I thought, was incomparably witty.

"I was a bit glum," I said, "because I was ruing how long everything takes. It's humiliating."

"What's humiliating?" The sun was in both our eyes. It was almost making me tear but it also was incredibly celebratory.

"You know, how long it takes to learn . . . anything . . ." I hesitated. "Play the hand you've been given, so to speak."

"You are an attractive woman," he answered, "so surely you've got plentiful chances. Or cards."

I nodded and said nothing. No assent but more importantly no defense.

"Come for a coffee," he said definitively, standing up. "After all, this is Vienna."

I looked at him and smiled. I liked his alertness. He was active, ready to be involved with the moment. Sure of himself, a bit like Oskar but with maybe, maybe a braver heart.

He picked the best section of the Café Mozart in the Hotel Sacher. Back here again. The sunlight came through the floor to ceiling windows. He confidently ordered us what he said were the best cakes there.

I looked at the tourists around us from Poland, Germany, Japan. The young couples with such clear skin holding each other's hands.

"Everybody gets hit, hurt at some time. We all make mistakes. Love the wrong person or work. No one's smarter. Then once you make a mistake," he said, "you move onto the next set of cards you're dealt."

I looked up at his strong face, longish grey hair, trim body. He had long fingers, as if he was a musician.

Two of Jean's three husbands, she herself and her daughter all underwent deprivation. La Santé, other prisons, a concentration camp. Obviously they all had to start over with nothing.

There's no shame in it.

"It took me two broken women, albeit geniuses, to wake me up to life . . ." I said to the philanthropist.

"Well then, here I am, sitting with a woken up woman, enjoying your quick eyes and your unusual dancing walk, and I get to wake up too."

Was he flirting with me?

"You have a wife," I said. "I saw her at the *Missa Solemnis*. Very beautiful."

"No I don't."

"Oh."

"That was my sister. She is beautiful apparently. Although, I can't see it. She's always complaining about something."

I laughed and looked out the window. God, things were amazing if you got out of your own way.

Jean and Marguerite, small and bright, stood at the window smiling.

He sat back. He was playing with his Blackberry.

"What are you doing?" I asked.

"Making us dinner reservations," he said.

"Do you know . . ." I asked, "Marguerite Duras?"

"Who?"

Well you can't get everything, I thought.

"She's a writer," I said. "Years after the war, after marriages, children, divorces, books, Duras' first lover, whom she had written about, came to Paris with his wife. He phoned her. She wrote in *The Lover*, '*It's me. She recognized him at once from the voice. He said, I just wanted to hear your voice. She said, it's me, hello. He was nervous, afraid, as before. His voice suddenly trembled. And with the trembling, suddenly, she heard again the voice of China. He knew she'd begun writing books, he'd heard about it through her mother whom he'd met again in Saigon. And about her younger brother, and he'd been grieved for her. Then he didn't know what to say. And then he told her. Told her that it was as before, that he still loved her, he could never stop loving her, that he'd love her until death.*' "

"Oh," the philanthropist said, uncomprehending but interested, curiously interested.

I caught myself all of a sudden acting like a girl. I was sort of leaning on the table, resting my head on my hand, my head tilted, looking up at him delighted. I was smiling as I looked at him. I liked his voice, it had energy and it was warm.

We began to get into a nonsensical discussion about forgetting words and I said, "I was once having breakfast and I could not remember the word for . . ." and then I couldn't remember it again, "it's *pamplemousse* in French . . ."

"Grapefruit?"

"No . . . it's tart, I don't like it . . ."

"Pineapple," he said quickly. "You mean *ananas*."

"Yes. That's right."

"I used to never like them either and now I do," he said.

Such a ridiculous conversation that I was enjoying. But I liked that he did not make fun of me, as Oskar would. He was sympathetic about my forgetting. It might mean he could be sympathetic about me being me. That would be the kind of person one could be with, for a long time.

"Well there's this new restaurant done by some architect, I can't remember his name speaking of forgetting things but, no, let's go there another time," he said, back to his Blackberry.

I nodded an assent, rather happily. He'd said, "another time."

Then he looked up and studied me for a bit. He had a funny way of turning slightly to listen, as if one ear was better than the other. It was endearing.

"I can pick you up later," he said. "How will you get home now?"

"I am home."

He looked at me confused. "What do you mean?"

"I lived here for a bit. It feels like home."

"At the Hotel Sacher?"

I nodded.

"How on earth . . .?"

"It doesn't have much to do with earth," I answered. "Anyway now I live about twenty blocks away."

"Very unspecific," he said.

"It is."

"I'll meet you here then at 7. You're not married are you?"

"No."

He stood up. "Good. Shall I walk you?"

I wanted him to so I could be with him longer and I didn't want him to because wanting to be with him was to kick up my longings and it felt too soon for either of us to be dealing with those.

We stood out in front of the café and we leaned in to kiss each other goodbye and I fell into his chest but non-committedly, because I didn't want to appear too hungry, so we kissed each other on the cheek. Well that is appropriate, I said to myself. We're not teenagers. We know how this all can end up. How the chances of it working are miniscule. But the real reason I didn't kiss him on the lips was because I felt shy.

THIRTY-ONE

Weeks had passed and I had started to find work here and there, editing manuscripts and the like, and so I moved out of Gerhardt's. Like the women before me had done in his life. The pain from his past lived with him too much and it felt claustrophobic. He was the type who wanted to keep an eye on his woman continually, even every fleeting thought of hers. Or maybe I knew everything he was going to say. Or maybe I preferred the unexpected.

Or maybe I now believed in love again. I liked seeing the philanthropist but he did not overly pursue me or call often. He had trips. He had commitments. He had this, that. I surmised maybe he even had a girlfriend he neglected to mention. When we saw each other, it was always languorously pleasant. Long dinners, an energy between us, but we never took that step to become one.

I was working all the time to make ends meet, just as I had been in New York but I suppose that is life. People passed my name around for people who wanted to write books about themselves and there is no limit of people wanting to write books about themselves and who am I to judge that?

Sometimes they wanted me to do the writing of the books about themselves. That was draining but fascinating to see such deep hope in people and how it manifested. To see how people wanted to be a story to themselves, one that they believed would teach others.

Often I did the writing sitting outside in the morning in a café. Delivery trucks would pass me. Men wearing glasses would walk by. Women walked by too but more slowly. Dogs would stop to sniff my legs. I thought, I must write outside more often. It makes me happy.

What would I write next of my own? I wasn't worried. I always seemed to have, aging or not, enough eros to keep going. But first I needed to work. I picked up the manuscript I was to edit about a man who was sexually infecting people as a payback for having been infected himself. Why did someone want to spend 300 pages writing about evil? Well, mine is not to reason, mine is to make a living.

After I spent some time on that, I moved onto editing a paper about the future of media. Facebook won't be anything as we see it now. Everything is online, crowdsourcing. People will sell by community approval. I was hardly interested. I sipped my coffee. The sun was out. Two old ladies with bicycles were talking across from me. Oh no, they walked away and the bicycles were left standing locked up next to a tree, belonging to other people. One woman had a cane. A reminder, a reminder to live and love now.

I switched to email on my Blackberry. From the philanthropist! How exciting. He is going to New York on Sunday for business. I wrote him back, "Maybe I will drive you to the airport."

Why am I being so forward? I don't even have a car. Not to mention know how to get to the airport. Hopefully he will say no. Or if he says yes, I will rent a car.

Ah, he replied. He doesn't know when he is going. I wrote back, Don't worry about it.

I was struck that he obfuscated. He was elusive. Even more so than Oskar had been, but the philanthropist and I are not yet lovers. He too is frightened. Or maybe it is my age. They no longer rush you as if from a burning fire to the bedroom.

But it was wonderful to feel that burst of enthusiasm, even if it was only my own enthusiasm.

I returned to the 100-page document on media, trying to find something, anything compelling. Well, I was learning about the world.

There was a slight breeze. I pushed on.

Marguerite sat down next to me. I moved my CDs and flowers . . . and then moved the papers for her.

She was dressed exactly as when I first met her.

I got a lump in my throat.

"I would not hesitate to ask, if I were you, for help from people," she said. "If they want your time, charge enough for it. And your next creative venture, ask to be remunerated. This nonsense of the struggling artist. We should get paid."

I nodded.

She smiled, "I know you don't like to call upon people. But you could try."

"As if you ever did."

"Completely untrue," she huffed. "I asked Dionys to help me when I needed money. Men like it fundamentally, to be needed. It makes them a man. I asked publishers to take on my work. I was always asking."

I nodded.

"If they say no, so what? At least you are your own advocate."

"Are you going somewhere?" I asked.

"This was all a bit exhausting," she said crossing her legs. She lit a cigarette and looked off, blindly almost.

"I am almost beginning to feel the same way myself," I said. "Back at the salt mine." I held up my papers. And, truth was, even after all this, I was still sleeping alone.

"Did you learn anything?" she asked.

"Yes, to love," I said. "I mean I still sabotage it, as you just referred. I left Gerhardt—"

"Not a bad idea in that case."

"The philanthropist—"

"Who knows about him?" she said.

"Yes, he's a bit not around."

"Anyway, you seem more at ease with yourself," she said. "That is not bad."

"But," I hesitated, "I often think of dying too, you know."

"Why?" She still was looking out at the street, not at me.

"I feel I can't go on anymore so alone. Supporting myself so itinerantly or being loved dispassionately, which may be all you get with age."

"Rather than die why not be vulnerable enough to reach out to someone? Like you did with us. We took care of you. Now you can let others. Let them love you."

"Yes," I said.

We were silent for a bit. I thought, She's right. I might prefer dying to being vulnerable. But that's ridiculous. I am only fooling myself about this whole thing. The will to live is stronger than that.

"I'll be around," she said, pointing to my head.

"James Salter just referred to you in his last book. Everyone still talks about you. You'll survive," I said.

She shrugged.

"Don't starve," she said, "And any chances you get, I mean when you are interested, be passionate."

I nodded.

"Show your passions. There's nothing wrong with them."

I looked at her with tears in my eyes, and tried to touch her. I tried to touch her with all the passion I felt for how she had lived with such passion and love and consciousness and perfect sentences and anger and impossibility and an absolute fidelity to art.

I reached out with all that passion flowing between us and then I realized she was gone.

THIRTY-TWO

Jean was holding her martini, sitting back in the big taupe chair. The young Irish bartender had dropped us both off another drink. She wasn't even tipsy. I was no longer sipping mine since I would be insensible if I did.

"Quite a lovely trip we went on," I said.

"Yes, very. I enjoyed it immensely."

I got that lump again.

We sat in silence for a bit.

"What are you thinking about?" she asked.

"I keep thinking, I don't know why, that I am going to die soon."

"Well you are." Then she hesitated, "It's just a part of you wants to die right now. That's why you feel it. The part that is old. You think you're old in years but you're not really. Look at you running about everywhere. What's old is the loneliness. I don't know if it goes away but one can do some variations on the theme."

I nodded.

"Don't shy away so much from not being alone. Let people get close to you, as you did with us. They won't hurt you. We didn't."

"True."

"Anyway," I said, "I appreciate all the time you gave me."

"Yes. It was good."

I suddenly felt so sad there would be no new books by her. That was it. I had read them all. I was lucky to have got to know her somewhat, as much as one ever knows a writer. They always joke that writers are boring people because it all goes into the work. Who knows? I hadn't found her boring. Or maybe writers hide from others their true material. Whomever she had showed me was worth it.

"I'll be seeing you I guess . . .?" I said probingly.

She looked at me queerly, her white hair, her veined hands, her staring blue eyes and then she, too, disappeared.

THIRTY-THREE

I got up and left the dark bar, and began walking along a forlorn Great Jones Street because of the heat. The sun was going down. I shuffled towards my apartment, my head swirling a bit. My Blackberry rang and out of habit I looked at it. Oskar: What are we doing tomorrow night? What movie or jazz?

The Pavlovian dog I am, I replied: Let's go see *Museum Hours* movie at the IFC. I will get the tickets later.

Response: ok

Nothing else. Not even, What's it about? I often dragged him to art films that I could see him thinking, What the hell are we doing here?

I type: Are you mad at me?

And then he types me a poem, which says he is never mad at me in the dark, but mad at some judgment calls I make.

What are you referring to? I type back.

No answer.

There is never an answer when the question has emotional value in it. He can only be concrete.

Then I walk along, filling in for him in my mind all the things I am mad at myself about.

Then I thought, but wait a minute. My play is about to go up, my strange magical play, just as Marguerite had spent time adding to her oeuvre. Odd, that similarity. We are trying to work on a film, my director and I, just coincidentally as Marguerite had done, at my age. Not that I was emulating her consciously, there just seemed to be that synchronicity. I was finishing a book about a lost woman, just as Jean had spent her life writing about. Sure I am alone as they were but so what.

I told myself I should focus on how to make my ships come in, not about whatever Oskar is judgmental with me about.

The next night I was by myself because to be involved with Oskar is to be by myself. He was allegedly having dinner with his most recent chef.

I decided to go to Carnegie Hall.

As I stood at the wicket line, I learned the Prokofiev violin concerto was sold out. I made my way back out through the crowds and there stood a man in the crowd holding up a ticket.

"Are you trying to sell that?" I asked.

"Yes."

"How much?" I asked.

He was tall, and rather attractive. I began to be pleasant about the whole exchange. I smiled for a change. He wore glasses and a vest. He felt accessible as a person, not posturing.

He looked at me.

"It's free," he said.

"Really?"

"A piece of good fortune," he said. "I don't need the money."

"Well that is very kind and honest of you. Thank you."

I took the ticket. Sadly he did not ask me details about myself, as men would have done 30 years ago. They would have exchanged the ticket for a date.

I weathered the slight to my vanity and went back into the concert hall. It was a good seat, Row F. Not too close so that you only end up seeing the shoes the musicians are wearing but close enough to see their faces and the nuances of their movement.

I felt rather plush and happy in the red velvet chair, in the gold and cream colored magnificent hall. I should be grateful for the gifts I do get, I tell myself. Not always be so quick to lament what I don't have. It's really a character flaw. I looked inside the program to see what else was playing. Sadly it was a modern piece that I had misgivings about.

The concert hall lights dimmed and then the man who gave me the ticket suddenly sat down next to me. He gave me a knowing smile, as if to say, "You see?"

Not sure what he thought I saw.

"Hello," I said, "and thank you again."

And then, we both turned to face the stage, the conductor turned his back to us, the musicians lifted up their instruments, a second held, and then the music slowly began.

ABOUT THE AUTHOR

British born, Montreal raised, New York City honed, JACQUELINE GAY WALLEY, under the pen name GAY WALLEY, has been publishing short stories since 1988 and published her first novel, *Strings Attached*, with University Press of Mississippi (1999), which was a Finalist for the Pirates Alley/Faulkner Award and earned a Writer's Voice Capricorn Award and the Paris Book Festival Award. *The Erotic Fire of the Unattainable: Aphorisms on Love, Art and the Vicissitudes of Life* was published by IML Publications in 2007 and was reissued by Skyhorse Publishing 2015. This book, *The Erotic Fire of the Unattainable* was a finalist for the Paris Book Festival Award and from this, she wrote a screenplay for the film, *The Unattainable Story* (2016) with actor, Harry Hamlin, which premiered at the Mostra Film Festival in Sao Paolo, Brazil. Walley also wrote a screenplay for director Frank Vitale's docufiction feature film, *Erotic Fire of the Unattainable: Longing to be Found* (2020), which was featured in Brooklyn Film Festival, Sarasota Film Festival, Cinequest Film & Creativity Festival in San Jose, ReadingFilmFest, and American Fringe in Paris (2020). Her novel, *Lost in Montreal* (2013) was published by Incanto Press, along with the novel, *Duet*, which was written with Kurt Haber. Walley's e-books, *How to Write Your First Novel*, *Save Your One Person Business from Extinction*, and *The Smart Guide to Business Writing* are featured on Bookboon, as well as *How to Keep Calm*

and Carry on Without Money and *How to be Beautiful* available on Amazon. In 2013, her play *Love, Genius and a Walk* opened in the Midtown Festival, New York, and was nominated for 6 awards including best playwright, in 2018, it also played in London at The Etcetera Theatre above The Oxford Arms pub as well as at three other pub theatres. It is scheduled to open in 2021 in Theatro Techni in London. October 2021, Jacqueline Gay Walley's 6 novel *Venus as She Ages Collection: Strings Attached* (second edition, under her pen name, Gay Walley), *To Any Lengths*, *Prison Sex*, *The Bed You Lie In*, *Write She Said*, and *Magnetism*, is being launched worldwide through IML Publications, distributed by Ingram.

Since IML's humble erratic beginnings, the mascot, which has reverently danced across our newsletter, the watermarks of the website, the original interiors, and now these front and back pages, is a graphic symbol of the Kalahari San Bushmen's Trickster God, the praying mantis, who has forever—or for as long as they can remember—been inspiring the mythological stories of these First People who nomadically walk the earth whenever they can, as our nomad authors write their way through life.

CPSIA information can be obtained
at www.ICGtesting.com
Printed in the USA
FSHW010000121121
86104FS